Keyport Cthulhu

Expanded Edition

**Armand Rosamilia
Katelynn Rosamilia
Chuck Buda**

All stories copyright 2017 their respective authors

Edited by Jenny Adams

All rights reserved, including the right to reproduce this book or portions thereof in any form, including electronic format, except for purposes of review

Rymfire Books

**Cover © 2017 by Jeffrey Kosh
http://jeffreykosh.blogspot.com/**

http://armandrosamilia.com

armandrosamilia@gmail.com

Special Thanks to Katelynn Rosamilia, for the typing help and the idea that Unicorns and Cthulhu could live in perfect harmony

Chuck Buda, a super fan who became a super part of this work

Introduction

By Chuck Buda

Exposure to the works of H.P. Lovecraft is not a prerequisite in order to enjoy *Keyport Cthulhu*. The book stands on its own, providing tales of darkness and dread. However, having read Lovecraft as a young man, I appreciated the painstaking work Armand Rosamilia crafted into this piece of art.

Keyport Cthulhu is an homage, not only to Lovecraft, but to the small fishing village of Keyport, New Jersey. The parallels are striking. Ancient traditions born of seafaring towns. Dankly worn piers and narrow streets. Somber feelings of isolation juxtaposed with the endless waters of escape. Atmospheric palls thick enough to choke on. And of course, eerie prose encapsulated in a nightmarish tome.

Armand Rosamilia's ability to modernize Lovecraft's style provides accessibility to the Cthulhu mythos. The master's imagination is harnessed, preserving the elements while carving a new path. And still, the course is horrific. Armand brings us the elder gods via universal fears. The human psyche has never been so exposed.

When I discovered *Keyport Cthulhu* for myself, I devoured it several times. I corresponded with Mr. Rosamilia, pleading for a sequel. I begged him to consider revisiting the mythos. Proudly, I convinced the author to re-release this great work with a fresh set of eyes. And now, I humbly present you with the new edition, including such classics as "Ancient," "Cabal," "Rats in the Cellars" and of course, "Cthulhunicorn" co-written with his daughter, Katelynn. The author has added a new tale, "Lockbox," as a bonus to the reader (but more than likely as a way to get rid of me for pestering him), Armand Rosamilia has included two of my own stories set in his personal mythos.

Sit back, dim the lights and immerse yourself in the world of *Keyport Cthulhu* as Armand Rosamilia takes you on a journey through the depths of madness.

Will you be strong enough to make it back?

-Chuck Buda, Rosamilia & Lovecraft Adept

Introduction... Page 5

Ancient... Page 9

Barren... Page 31

Cabal... Page 65

Dagon... Page 91

Evil... Page 123

Rats In The Cellars... Page 163

Cthulhunicorn... Page 189

The Terrible Old Man of Keyport... Page 193

Lockbox... Page 215

Dark Waters of Sin... Page 239

Author Notes... Page 253

ANCIENT

"This entire town smells like fish," Nicole whispered to her husband as they sat in their car and waited for the realtor to arrive.

"You'll get used to it. Trust me." Harrison tapped on the BMW's steering wheel to the song in his head. "I haven't been here in years."

"It smells. It smells bad," she reiterated. "You promised me a vacation down the Jersey shore."

Harrison pointed at the bay. "There's a patch of beach right there."

Nicole squinted dramatically. "Where? Between the fish guts, the giant freaking seagulls and the strange fishermen on their hundred year old blocks of wood, I don't see anything that could be called sand."

"Trust me, you'll love it here."

"Love it here?" Nicole crossed her arms. "I don't think so. This was supposed to be a drive down from Boston to see and sell your grandfather's house. That was it."

"I promised you Snookie and a porkroll, egg and cheese sandwich, as well."

"That sounds gross, and so is Snookie. This is crap."

Harrison loved that she never used profanity. She would use heck or freaking or darn whenever she broke a nail or stubbed a toe. He was born in New Jersey (right down Route 36 in nearby Belford) and cursed like a fucking sailor. "I grew up here."

Nicole went back into her dramatics, while trying to stifle a grin. She threw her arms up, striking the car roof and the closed window. "You grew up in this swamp?"

"The swamps of Jersey, like the Boss sang about."

"Who's boss?"

Harrison laughed. He was about to explain the finer points of Bruce Springsteen and Bon Jovi music to this New England gal when a car horn honked next to her and an older woman, wearing too much makeup and a bright red smile, waved and pulled away.

"That must be the realtor slash clown of Keyport," Harrison said and started the car.

"You're horrible. That's not nice. She's someone's mother or daughter."

Nicole was always seeing the good in people, despite the fact that most of them were shit, in Harrison's mind. He'd been living in Fall River for the past ten years but couldn't shake the 'Jersey' out of him, and didn't ever want to. New Englanders made fun of his 'hey you's guys' and ending too many too-true comments with 'just sayin' and his other accents, but he could rib the Bahstahn accent as well. Pahk the Cah.

They caught up to the realtor on 1st Street and turned left onto Walnut. As they got back to the bay, they followed her right onto a dirt road, running parallel to the water. Stunted trees rose up on both sides, scratching the top of the car as they passed. Most of the trees to the east, near the water, were leaning precariously as if reaching for the salt water, the roots going to the waterline itself.

"Crazy trees," Nicole said and pointed at them. "This place is creepy."

Harrison tried to think of something funny to say but failed when they veered around a tree stump next to the road that looked like a troll or a monster. She was right; it was creepy.

The dust kicked up by the realtor's car obscured their view more than a few feet ahead of them, but when she suddenly turned to the right and stopped, Harrison hit his breaks and they waited for the dust to settle.

"1313 Mockingbird Lane," Harrison said with a laugh. "It's like a movie set, right?"

"I'm not getting out." Nicole crossed her arms.

* * * * *

Harrison stood on the cobblestone pathway leading to his late grandfather's house. The lawn - if you could even call it that - was just patches of brown weeds, ropy vines hugging the ground, and what looked to be mole or gopher mounds. The trees thinned out and he had a clear view of the bay to his left, although, he thought it would take awhile to actually walk to the slight beach if he wanted to.

He glanced back and waved at Nicole, still sitting in the car, but she looked away. He'd need to make this up to her with a great dinner and maybe a romantic stroll on the waterfront tonight. A few drinks wouldn't hurt, either.

The realtor, wearing a gaudy, brightly colored dress, smiled as she held the keys and stood on the top step. Her makeup threatened to slide off her face and Harrison had the funny vision of it doing so and taking her eyes, nose and lips with it.

"When was the last time you visited?" she asked.

Harrison shook his head as he looked over the outside of the house, weathered and gray, the wooden siding looking ancient. It was a huge house, two stories, with a gabled gray roof and drab accoutrements. It looked as if it had been washed of all real color, like a black and white picture. He joined her out of the direct sunlight and returned her fake smile. "I've never been here."

She looked surprised. "I thought you were born here?"

"Yeah, I'm a Jersey boy."

Now she looked agitated. "No, you misunderstand. On the phone, I thought you said you were born in Keyport."

"I was born in Red Bank and grew up in Belford."

She palmed the keys and Harrison watched the move, wondering if she was going to pocket them and leave. This is my fucking house now, bitch, he wanted to yell at her. He had no idea what he'd said wrong or if any of it was even her business.

"My mother was born here but left home at sixteen. To be honest, I don't think she ever spoke with her father after that. He creeped her out." Like the trees on the property, he suddenly thought.

Her smile returned and she jingled the keys. "I know of several Keyport residents who'd love to make this a quick sale."

"What do you mean?"

"Well, I know you live in New England and the only reason you got the property is because you're the only family Jeb Marsh had left." The realtor glanced at Nicole, still sitting in the car. "I don't mean to pry, but it's obvious your pretty little wife isn't too happy to be down here. I can take care of all the paperwork."

Harrison put his hand out and she handed him the keys. "I'm thinking of staying for awhile. I can do my work from the house. With today's business all being done online and through e-mails, I can work from anywhere. Does the house have an office set up?"

The realtor shrugged. "I've never been inside."

Harrison suddenly had a thought. "When I got the call originally, it was from a Mister Smoltz. Why isn't he meeting me here to give the keys?"

She smiled. "Mister Smoltz was your grandfather's lawyer and did all the paperwork, like his will, and got all of his finances, such as they are, in order."

"And?"

"I'm Sylvia. Sylvia Smoltz." She laughed, her chins jiggling. "My, how rude of me! I never properly introduced myself. I do most, if not all, of the real estate deals in Keyport." She leaned in closer to him. "Not that there are many. Most of the town is family, in one way or another, and a death usually means the property is simply handed down to a son or daughter or grandchild." She stopped smiling. "Of course, ninety-nine percent of the time the family member still lives in town or was born here. Where's your mother, anyway?"

Harrison was sweating in the heat and was done with the small talk and this annoying woman. He dropped his own smile and simply (but as nice as he could manage) took the keys from her chubby hand. "I'll be in touch with you if I decide to sell the place."

She went to say something but he turned his back to her, unlocked the front door and pushed it open. Harrison turned to make sure she left but she was almost running down the steps and down the path.

Nicole glanced at him irritably. When he gave her a little wave, she looked away. "This is going to be a fun night," he murmured.

He took a tentative step inside but didn't fully enter. His eyes began adjusting to the gloom and he marveled at the amount of dust swirling in the air.

Harrison's grandfather had only been dead ten days. Mister Smoltz had taken care of the burial and the paperwork, notifying Harrison only two days ago. Harrison would need to contact the lawyer again and get the location of his grandfather's gravesite.

The windows, in the front room, were covered in heavy curtains and the furniture draped in cloths. Harrison finally walked in and realized he'd been holding his breath.

The house had a strange smell to it, as if bleach had been dumped in the next room, but Harrison doubted anyone had cleaned in years. There was an underlying smell of... something else. Surprisingly, there were no pictures on the walls. If he didn't know better, he'd think no one had lived in the house for years.

Harrison moved into the living room, but tried not to disturb anything. It was like stepping back through time. He wandered down the hall into what served as a kitchen, although, the appliances hadn't been updated in the last fifty years.

Again, it was like a museum. There was dust on the kitchen table and on the counters. Nothing was out of place and the single window over the sink was covered with a gaudy black fabric.

"How is it possible that he's only been dead a few days?"

Harrison searched the rest of the bottom floor but the rooms were equally vacant and dusty. Half way up the steps, he pulled back a thick curtain, expecting to find a window, so he could check on Nicole.

The painting forced him to move back with such suddenness, he nearly fell over the side of the old wooden railing. It depicted a grizzly scene, as if your worst nightmare had been splattered on canvas. Despite his mind screaming to look away, he could not avert his eyes.

The myriad of colors, some of which he could not even name, seemed to pulse. Creatures, bent in some horrific struggle, moved from the corner of his eyes. When he looked directly at them, they were simply a jumble of obscene color.

Harrison felt his heart racing. He needed to get up the stairs, but his body was fighting him. He thought again of Nicole waiting for him in the car, and that seemed to give him strength. He literally had to put his hand over his eyes to break the spell.

At the top of the stairs, he realized he been holding his breath.

He leaned against the wall and waited for his heart beat to slow. The second level contained five closed doors. Again, no pictures adorned the hallway walls. He opened the closest door and wasn't surprised to find it the same. He walked across the dusty floor, put a trembling hand on the black fabric covering what he hoped was a window, and closed his eyes.

He yanked the drape down and felt sunlight on his face. Looking outside, he saw that Nicole was no longer in the car. At the same moment, he heard the front door slam closed.

"Honey, I'm up here." Harrison said, going to the landing and looking down but he didn't see her. "Nicole?"

Something heavy fell in the far room down the hall. Harrison hesitated. Should he go downstairs and look for Nicole, who should be fuming by now, or investigate the noise down the hall?

Another crash sounded and Harrison ran to the door and tried to open it. It was locked and made of solid wood, old and ancient, but the lock itself looked brand new. What was also odd was the large padlock at the top of the door.

Harrison pulled the keys from his pocket but none of them fit in the padlock. The newest looking key unlocked the door itself, so he turned the knob and pushed it no more than a quarter inch before the padlock held.

Something slammed against the other side of the door with such force that Harrison fell backwards and the floor actually shuddered.

That's when he heard Nicole scream from below.

* * * * *

She stood on top of one of the kitchen chairs, tears streaming down her face.

"Oh my god, what happened?" Harrison stopped in the door way when he saw Nicole.

Nicole sobbed and pointed at the sink. "There's a giant rat."

Harrison couldn't help but laugh, relieved at the explainable problem. When Nicole got down off the chair and gave him the finger, he moved to hug her. She pushed him away.

"I'm just messing with you," Harrison said as he tried to hug his wife again. She resisted. "Why are you such a jerk? You know rats freak me out."

"It was probably a field mouse. I'm sure this ancient house is a breeding ground for them."

Nicole pushed past him and he followed her out the front door, managing to stop her on the porch. "I'll get an exterminator in the morning. I think we have a bigger problem upstairs."

"What do you mean?"

"Something big is pissed off and living in one of the bedrooms. It's either a raccoon or a huge squirrel."

Harrison grinned. "Maybe it was a unicorn."

"Maybe you're an idiot."

Harrison shrugged. "I'm starving. Let's go into town and find an early dinner and some beer."

* * * * *

"This is a nice place," Harrison said and looked around the small bar. It was dark and they sat at the only table that wasn't occupied, although, most of the room was taken up by the bar area and the pool tables and dart throwing area.

Nicole frowned. She glanced around the bar before looking back at her husband. "Do I have something on my face?"

"No." Harrison was confused.

Nicole leaned closer to Harrison. "Then why the heck is everyone staring at us?"

Harrison met the gaze of several men at the bar, expecting them to look away.

Instead, they continued to stare. The room was quiet, all eyes on the couple.

"Let's just get out of here." Nicole stood and moved to the door and Harrison almost had to run to keep up.

"Ready to order?" It was the bartender asking, standing with his arms folded and a smirk on his face. He didn't look too friendly, weathered like everyone else they'd met in Keyport in their short stay so far. Harrison felt like he was in a foreign country.

Nicole had stopped in the doorway. Harrison took his wife gently by the arm and took her outside, glad when the door closed. He was sure he heard laughter inside.

"Let's just get in the car and drive home," Nicole said.

Harrison took his wife's hands in his. He knew this hadn't turned out how he'd planned. *I guess I fooled myself into thinking my New England born and bred wife would fall in love with the area I grew up in. Unfortunately, this isn't where I grew up*, he thought, as they stood on the corner of Broad Street and Main.

"I say we go to the realtors first thing in the morning, list that creepy house and get out of this creepy town. With the money you'll make off of it, we can buy our own house near Boston. I have cousins in Fall River." Nicole checked her watch. "If you let me drive, we can be home before midnight."

Harrison was annoyed even though he knew, on a rational level, his wife was right. He didn't know what he thought he'd actually find here. His mother had always been a mystery to him, and he was really raised by his father's side of the family. When the realtor asked about his family today, it was really none of her business. Truth be told, he hadn't seen his mother since his 13th birthday. He knew his parents were getting divorced, remembering that his mother had been *reborn* with some hokey religion. Most nights he went to sleep with a pillow over his ears because his father ridiculed her talk of sea creatures and sleeping gods.

"Hello?" Nicole said to her husband, bringing him back to the present.

"Sorry, I'm just really hungry and this day has been crap. Look, from what I have heard, there's a great seafood place just down the road. What do you say I treat you to a romantic dinner of fried fish while we sit in the parking lot and watch the sun go down?"

Nicole hooked her arm in his. "Seafood? Really? I've never had seafood before. I was only born in New England."

Harrison had to laugh. "I guess that would be like trying to impress someone from Baltimore with crab cakes."

"Or like trying to impress someone from Tijuana with Mexican food."

"Or trying to sell ice cubes to Eskimos."

Nicole playfully punched him in the arm. "That's racist. You can't call them Eskimos."

"Then what do you call them?"

Nicole shrugged." Beats me. I'm from New England. Let's go try this amazing seafood from New Jersey."

* * * * *

They pulled up to the ancient house an hour after dark. There were no street lights, and Harrison had forgotten to put the porch light on. The only illumination came from the water, possibly a ship.

Harrison opened his car door but didn't get out when Nicole made no move to follow.

"Honey, we went over this at dinner. The only smart thing to do is to stay here tonight. We can't afford a hotel room, and I swear I'll call the realtor tomorrow to sell the house. I admit I brought you with me thinking that you'd fall in love with the house." Harrison smiled sheepishly. "I guess I had the romantic notion of living near the water and getting back to my roots."

"You already live near the water, in a modern house with modern appliances and without a vermin problem."

Harrison put up his index finger. "One night, and I swear we head back to Boston. The next time we visit will be to sign the final papers, and visit Snookie."

Nicole opened her door and smiled. "Fine. One night in the Munster house won't kill me, but you can forget about seeing the sleepwear I packed."

"That's not fair." Harrison got out and moved to the trunk of the car. "I suppose I have to get all the bags now?"

Nicole snapped her finger. "Hurry up, bellboy."

Harrison struggled with the luggage. "Ma'am, tipping is required in this establishment."

Nicole grabbed two bags herself and laughed. They walked up the steps and he fumbled with the keys in the dark. When he finally found the right key and opened the door, he set the bags just inside the doorway. Reaching around in the dark, he finally located a light switch but when he flipped it nothing happened. Nicole moved past him inside.

"Is the power out?"

A lamp suddenly turned on in the room. Nicole, with a grin, had a hand on the lamp. "Look, magic! You hit the button on the lamp and it creates light."

"Sarcasm will get you nowhere." Harrison picked up two of the suitcases but as he looked up the stairs he shivered. Did he just now hear a bang against a door or was that his imagination?

Nicole grabbed the rest of the luggage and put a foot on the bottom step. "I'm guessing there's a bedroom up there? It seems kind of freaky to be sleeping in your grandfather's bed. Did you see if there was a guest room?"

Harrison put down the suitcases next to the door and took the bags from his wife and put them back.

"What are you doing?"

Harrison did not want to go upstairs. He only checked one room but knew that the rest of them were also devoid of furniture. The padlocked room might contain a bed but it was probably occupied. *By what...* Harrison decided he didn't want to know. "You know what, honey? Let's just get a hotel."

He could see Nicole was both aggravated and tired. She sat down on the second step. "You're joking, right?"

Harrison knew how close he was to completely pissing her off. But right now, you couldn't give him a million dollars to walk up those steps. "There's nowhere to sleep upstairs."

"Are you f-... freaking kidding me? Why wouldn't you tell me hours ago that there was nowhere to sleep?" She was getting hot. Heck, she'd almost cursed. While she often chided him on his Jersey attitude and short temper, she was his polar opposite.

Harrison turned and tried his best to fake a smile as he looked into the living room. "I have a fun idea. Why don't we crash on the couches? It will be like in college when you slept on the futon." He went over to the lamp that she turned on and moved it onto the dusty coffee table, hoping it would make the room brighter and more inviting. He noticed the key for a small lock half buried in the dust on the coffee table and put it in his pocket, hoping Nicole didn't notice.

She wasn't happy. Harrison took a step back, waiting for the explosion. "There's a Ramada in Hazlet we could drive to and be in the room in less than half an hour."

Nicole muttered under her breath as she grabbed luggage and headed out the door. Harrison scooped up the remaining bags and followed. As he turned to shut the door, he was sure he heard a bang from upstairs.

Halfway down the path, the wind picked up and he knew it was going to rain soon.

"Fuck!" Nicole yelled, standing next to the trunk of the car. Harrison dropped the suitcases and ran to her. "What's the matter?" She'd screamed with such fury at first he thought she'd been bitten by a snake.

Nicole had a hand over her mouth, whether if in embarrassment or shock, Harrison didn't know. When she pointed at the two deflated rear tires, he wanted to curse himself.

Harrison did when he saw the two front tires were also slashed. As if in answer to his blasphemy, the sky opened up and it began to pour.

Without a word, and not meeting the gaze of his wife, Harrison managed to grab all of the bags and trudge through the rain and back onto the porch.

He was about to comment on the lights coming from the water, seemingly a dozen different points out in the bay. Instead, he opened the door and silently followed Nicole inside making sure the door was locked.

* * * * *

Nicole's stiff neck woke her up and she rolled off the couch and onto all fours with a start. Even in the dark of the living room, she was sure a dust cloud had been stirred. Harrison snored softly on the other couch.

They'd gone to sleep fighting. Nicole was frustrated at this entire trip and wanted to punch her husband in the face. She'd lost her cool too many times today and it was something she never did. Ever. She grimaced at the thought of using such a vile word when she saw the tires slashed.

It was raining outside and she could hear water dripping in the hallway. Nicole was sure there was more than one hole in the ancient roof, and wouldn't be surprised if a solid rain would flood out a room or two.

She needed to use the bathroom. Nicole didn't want to turn on the light, but she had no idea whether it was downstairs or upstairs. She smiled and had an idea.

Her cell phone was in her small purse, and she could use the light of it to see.

Only the phone wasn't there. She checked her jeans, wadded on the floor and then around the coffee table and chairs.

"Please, don't let the phone still be in the car," she whispered.

Why hadn't she simply gone to the bathroom before sleep? She glanced at her snoring husband and knew why: because she was mad as heck and made sure she got undressed in front of him, but didn't even give him a kiss goodnight before plopping onto a couch, ignoring the cloud of dust, and twisting her body away from him.

Harrison had tried to talk with her but she kept telling him to leave her alone and let her sleep, and he'd finally obeyed and shut up. The heavier rain had come then and, even if they'd wanted to talk, the noise as it bounced off the ancient house would have precluded that.

Nicole knelt next to her husband. She whispered his name softly to see if he was deep into sleep, although, his snoring had gotten louder in the last minute. He'd fallen asleep with his clothes still on, even his sneakers. She slid two fingers in his right front pocket searching for his phone. She found it. When she carefully slid the phone out of his pocket, something metallic clanged to the floor.

It was a small key, one she'd never seen before in her husbands' possession.

She walked out of the living room and halfway up the stairs before stopping. Flipping open his phone, she used the light to get a better look at the key.

Her bathroom break was now forgotten, as she heard something heavy drop upstairs.

Should I wake Harrison? She used the cell phone like a flashlight, pointing it in front of her as she navigated the steps in her bare feet. At the landing, she stopped and looked around. The hall was empty and all the doors were closed. As she moved the cell phone around, she caught a glimmer of something at the far end.

Nicole hesitated. Her mind screamed to wake her husband. She took three tentative steps and stopped, listening to the rain as it bounced around above her in the attic.

She had the insane thought to rush down the steps, wake Harrison and tell him that the rain was destroying the house and the property value.

She heard a tap on the far door and couldn't help but approach. There was a padlock just within reach at the top of the door, and she was positive she had the key to it.

There was another tap on the other side of the door.

"Hello?" Nicole whispered.

When she heard the crying, she jabbed the key in the lock. As the padlock fell to the dusty hallway floor, the door swung inward and she noticed the pair of red eyes.

* * * * *

Harrison woke with a start, the front door wide open and the wind gusting rain into the foyer. He leapt from the couch but before he got two steps he realized his wife wasn't sleeping on the other couch. He went to the door and poked his head out but the rain was sluicing off the battered porch roof and through so many holes it looked like a shower. He called for Nicole but the noise of the weather drowned him out.

That was when he realized his cell phone was no longer in his pocket and the padlock key was missing.

Harrison stared up the dark steps in fear. He put his right foot tentatively on the first step. As if in reply, the house shook from a clap of thunder.

Don't think, just move. Nicole is up there. He knew beyond a shadow of a doubt that his wife was in trouble. Harrison felt like he'd failed her.

He turned his brain off, willed his feet to move, and ran to the top of the stairs. Even though it was so dark that he couldn't see his hand in front of his face, he knew what door he needed to get to.

Harrison cried out when he kicked the padlock, somewhere on the ground in the hall. He put his hands out blindly and began to sob when he realized the door was open.

"Nicole?"

She wasn't in the room and whatever had been here was now gone. It felt... anticlimactic. Harrison suddenly felt hollow inside.

He began screaming for his wife.

He was down the stairs, out the front door, and running-sliding across the lawn, his throat raw from screaming in a losing battle with the weather.

In seconds he was soaked. He could actually feel his mind slip. Hysterical, he was running toward the bay. Nicole was there, somewhere out there among the lights.

Even through the sheets of driving rain, he could see the boats. Like a procession, the rowboats and small craft moved single file away from land.

Harrison didn't know if he was seeing things. He didn't know if his mind had snapped or was showing him an imagined horror.

Despite the distance and poor visibility, Harrison swore he saw Nicole standing in the front of a rowboat and embracing a grotesque albino before the two figures plunged overboard.

* * * * *

Harrison stood on the porch and watched as the realtor pulled up next to his car. As she exited, she put a hand on her sizable chin. "Wow, what happened to your tires?"

Harrison was silent, just watching as she approached.

"I brought the papers with me." She took a jumble of papers from her satchel and tried to hand them and a pen to Harrison.

Harrison didn't move to take it, so she finally put everything down on one of the drier parts of the porch.

"Tell me, where is my grandfather buried? I never did ask."

The realtor looked away. "I need you to sign the papers. I have a buyer lined up." She glanced at his car. "I'll call a really good mechanic in town and he'll run over four new tires. That way you can be home before dark."

Harrison picked up the paper work. "I am home." He scattered the papers on the porch.

"You don't seem to understand..." she began to say but Harrison put a finger up and she stopped.

"Oh, I do understand. I understand all of it now."

As Harrison began trudging though the mud following the tracks from last night made by his wife and grandfather, he wondered how fast he could find a rowboat.

BARREN

Three weeks ago he was called Bones, sporting a long red goatee and ponytail, proudly flying the black and silver of the Black Death Motorcycle gang (nomads based in Florida), cruising on his 1200 Low Harley bike, and surrounded by his brothers.

He pulled into the parking lot of the Keyport Diner in a stolen Honda Civic and parked it in the darkest corner he could find, near the dumpster. He wore his black riding gloves but wiped down the steering wheel, doors and dashboard before grabbing his backpack and exiting, leaving the keys in the ignition.

Now he was known as Bobby Anderson (according to his new ID), and his head and face were clean shaven. Gone were his earrings, his colors and his bike. He wore a non-descript gray T-shirt, blue jeans and a pair of sneakers. Even his Harley sunglasses and chain wallet had been replaced by cheap WalMart versions with no markings or corporate logos. Bobby Anderson was your average, anonymous, forty-ish guy passing through. And right now he just wanted an endless cup of weak coffee with a cheeseburger and fries.

The counter was filled with teens and those still in their twenties, making a racket. Bones—shit, Bobby, from now on Bobby—slid into a booth by himself, the empty one in the far corner, allowing him to see the doors and put his back to something solid. It was Friday night and he supposed there was a movie theatre or bowling alley or someplace the local riffraff hung out before hitting the diner with their change and holding onto a drunken night. Those Friday nights seemed to be in his rearview mirror right now.

The waitress was ten years past being anything to look at but she smiled when she took his order, lingering at his table like she wanted to say something flirty or witty. He'd leave exactly fifteen percent on the tip, not make small talk, and hope she'd forget about him in an hour or two.

Shit. Two shields, State troopers, walked in and smiled at the hostess while scanning the diner like good cops did.

Bobby yawned casually and picked up the greasy dessert menu, his eyes watching the two as they were led to the only other empty booth in the diner. The one next to his.

He casually leaned back and made sure his Ruger LCP 380 ACP was hidden, tucked in his waistband. The last thing he wanted was a shootout in a diner with two troopers. His coffee came and he added a ton of cream and sugar to it, finishing it in two gulps.

The waitress turned to the shields and took their order. Bobby continued to study the dessert menu while listening to their conversation. He'd heard the nearest cop, the bald one, say something about a murder when he put his cover on the seat next to him.

The other trooper, a skinny guy with glasses, was leaning forward and talking louder than normal to be heard over the kids at the counter. "Damn if I can figure it out. My brother Nate says six bodies have washed up in the last three days."

"Six more?" Bald Cop asked. "How many does that make it?"

Bobby watched Skinny Cop shrug. "I don't talk to him much, but they have a clusterfuck going on in Sunken City."

"Glad I don't work down there. This stretch of Route 36 is busy enough with drunk drivers and speeders. I don't want to mess with dead bodies." Bald Cop smiled when the waitress dropped his coffee cup and a buttered bagel in front of him.

Bobby didn't know where Sunken City was and didn't care.

Maybe there was a shipwreck off the coast, or a storm he missed had killed a family? None of his business and he didn't plan on staying in New Jersey that much longer. His next move would be to hole up in a cheap cash-only motel for the night and then hitch a ride north and get as close to Upstate New York as possible. The greater the distance between him and his former brothers in Black Death, the better.

"They really think it's a serial killer?" Bald Cop asked.

That piqued Bobby's interest. A serial killer was one of those things you read about or saw on the news after the fact. If they were in the grip of an honest to God mass murderer, someone who maybe tortured people or was a cannibal… shit, that would be cool. He'd never met that kind of celebrity before.

Skinny Cop was talking around a mouthful of bagel. "Each of the victims was missing a weird part of their body. One had a hand missing, another had one less ear."

"How do they know it wasn't just the fish eating the ear off?"

"I heard the cut was perfect in each case. Like that murder in Long Branch last year, where the guy killed those people on that vacant lot off of Chelsea Avenue."

Bald Cop laughed. "So glad you don't know too much."

"I'm a good cop; I can't help being thorough with my knowledge."

Even though both cops were laughing, there was truth in his words. Bobby *knew* they were both on the up and up. He could *sense* it. Some called it a gift. He called it the only thing that kept him alive.

Since he was a child he'd been able to read people. Not their thoughts but their character. He didn't exactly understand it, even now. He just knew looking at certain people whether or not they were genuine or lying or deadly. It only worked on about a quarter of the people he'd met in his life, and usually it was only the extreme emotional ones that he could read easily.

Like the guy in the opposite corner that was also watching the two officers. He was... *bad*. Real bad. One of those guys you got sick about if you stared at him too long. Bobby tried to turn away but he couldn't, even when the man sighted on him and locked eyes.

There was something wrong about him. Like he wore a mask, his boring features covering a demon. Bobby was an integral part of Black Death (was, he reminded himself) because of this gift, reading certain people and letting the other guys know what was about to go down. He couldn't tell the future and didn't get visions, but he got what he knew as hunches.

His hunch right now was this guy was evil.

Bobby's fingers on his right hand were going numb and he realized he'd been gripping the backpack on the seat next to him with such ferocity his fingers were white.

"Another cup, sugar?" It was the waitress and she broke Bobby's grip on the backpack and his thoughts, slapping him back to reality. He looked at her, locked eyes, and tried to concentrate on her face and slow his accelerated heart rate.

"Huh?" he managed.

She held a steaming pot of coffee up and smiled. "Need some more?" When he nodded, she slowly filled his coffee cup, leaning further than was necessary, her generous chest now eye level for his perusal. "What else can I get you?"

Bobby shook his head but couldn't help staring. He was a guy after all. "Just my burger and fries."

She laughed and pointed at the table. "Cutie, your food has been in front of you for ten minutes. It's probably cold now."

"Shit." Bobby smiled sheepishly. "Daydreaming again." He put his head down in embarrassment and picked up his cheeseburger, no longer hungry.

"You want me to heat it up for you?"

"No, thanks." He took a bite without looking at the waitress. He didn't want her to remember he was there in the event something happened to him or to someone else, but he knew he'd blown that by being an airhead.

On his third bite of the cold burger, she reluctantly wandered away to another table. When Bobby looked up the State Troopers were gone, their table now occupied by drunken teenagers. The scary guy in the corner was also gone, and Bobby knew that wasn't a coincidence. There was a connection between him and the cops and the bodies washing ashore in Sunken City (wherever that was) but he didn't want to figure it out; he had his own shit to deal with. He was on the run for a reason, and there were thirteen bad-ass motorcycle motherfuckers looking for him and this backpack.

The waitress was back just as he stuffed the last two French fries in his mouth and sipped the last of the coffee. When he didn't make eye contact with her, she put the check on the table and walked away. He put cash on the table, tipping her twenty percent and walking out. Bobby had no idea where he was going, but it was getting late, he was on foot, and he had a bad feeling in his gut. He gripped the backpack and started walking east down Broad Street.

* * * * *

Bobby found himself sitting on a weathered pylon staring at the dark bay and east. He'd guessed east was the way into the center of town, but didn't realize there were no hotels on the main strip, or anywhere to rent a room for the night. He felt like he was in a town that time had forgotten: the street lights were ancient-looking, the buildings simple and uniform, one after another on the main drag. He didn't see any chain stores on his way down the road. There was no Blockbuster, just a tiny place called Whateley Movie Rentals, but as Bobby glanced in the window it looked to be filled with VHS cassettes. It was like walking down a street in 1988.

Shoe repair, mom and pop clothing and shoe stores, and the one bar he saw—Broad Street Pub—told him he wouldn't be eating McDonalds or drinking Dunkin Donuts coffee in the morning.

There was Keyport Fishery right across the parking lot but it was closed at this time of night. The only thing outside with him was a stray seagull, watching him warily from the other side of the lot. The dock was empty of ships, and Bobby assumed they were out shrimping or fishing or whatever they caught in New Jersey.

Right now, he didn't care. He needed a place to crash and didn't feel like sleeping outdoors; although, it was better than being caught... he put a hand on the backpack and pulled it closer.

A car's headlights bounced around the buildings near him and he ducked down, watching as a BMW came around the road in front of the docks slowly. *Are they already looking for me? Have they found me that quickly?* Bobby wasn't the only one with powers in the Black Death MC gang. Hell, everyone in the crew had a special gift. And some of those were being used to find him, he had no doubt.

He had nowhere to actually hide unless he jumped over the bulwark into the bay, and he didn't want to do that. The salty smell of the water was strong and he had a crazy notion, if he jumped in, he'd be covered in barnacles, seaweed and a slimy green color that he'd never be able to wash off. The waves suddenly felt ominous, drumming against the wall below him, reaching up to grip him and pull him into their depths...

When the BMW slowed to a crawl at the far end of the parking lot, directly in front of the Keyport Fishery, he hoped it was a coincidence. Maybe it was the first shift for the fishery. He was sure they had to get there in the middle of the night when the ships pulled in with the shrimp or scallops or whatever they caught out there.

Bobby was squatting against the short wall behind him, ready to spring away. The BMW was now stopped, headlights shining right at him. He was in a spotlight, caught. He turned sideways with his right hand gripping the Ruger LCP 380 ACP tucked into the back of his pants.

If he had to, he'd kill someone, but only if there was no way around it. His goal was still to make no waves, leave no impression in this little town, and be on his way before Black Death found his trail. Shooting someone would leave a psychic *mark* that Tank could easily find. Between the twelve biker brothers he'd screwed over and left behind, Tank was the one he feared most. There was no one more loyal, but once you crossed the line you were dead to him. And soon you actually were dead. Bones (fuck, Bobby... Bobby) had witnessed it with his own eyes and helped Tank bury a few people that got on his wrong side.

The headlights went off and on quickly, three times, in quick succession. Bobby drew the weapon slowly but kept it out of sight, against his hip. The only sound was the BMW engine across the parking lot and his own controlled breathing.

When the car began to move, Bobby braced himself to spring and mentally focused his attention to figure out where his first two shots were going: the windshield at the driver's head and the front right tire. But the car swung around and drove away quickly, out of the parking lot, heading north without braking at two stop signs before its tail lights disappeared around a building.

Bobby started walking south with no real destination in mind, although, he knew staying here at the docks was a mistake. As he crossed back onto Broad Street, he passed a bar with its door open, probably airing out after a long night.

A bald man was just inside the doorway, white shirt covered in dark liquid, arms folded and staring intently as Bobby went by.

Bobby got a chill and picked up the pace.

"You lost, buddy?" the man yelled from behind.

Bobby stopped and turned slowly, aware he still had the gun in his hand. He tucked it in his waistband, hoping the darkness hid it. "Excuse me?"

The man was now halfway out the door of the establishment, still standing with crossed arms. He didn't say another word but his look was disconcerting. Bobby got the bad impression that this man knew more than he should.

"What?" Bobby finally said and waved his arms. His bad feeling was back, and this guy was trouble. Bobby didn't want anything to do with him or his bar. He turned and walked briskly away, glancing back every few steps.

The man stayed in the doorway with folded arms and simply stared.

* * * * *

Bobby didn't know what denomination the church was. It was still a couple of hours before first light, and he needed to at least get a nap in. He could feel his body fighting him to shut down. If trouble found him (and several times already tonight it felt close), he needed his full strength.

The building was set back from the road on a corner property with the graveyard surrounding on all sides. There was no light on anywhere, and the street lights in the area were all out. Bobby looked closer and saw the two closest bulbs had been shattered, the pieces still in the road.

The church and surrounding area looked almost abandoned and Bobby's senses tingled. Something was definitely wrong, like an ominous black cloud hung over the church. He was just about to turn away and find another refuge when the front light on the entryway came on, a sickly yellow bulb that only cast light a few feet down the path.

As the front doors of the church opened slowly, Bobby pulled the gun but pointed it at the ground, expecting something bad to attack him.

But his feelings of danger dropped when the old priest came onto the first step and squinted into the darkness. "Is someone there?"

Bobby felt relief flooding over him and he stepped forward, dragging his feet so the priest could hear his approach. "Good evening, Father." He put the gun away.

The priest looked frightened until Bobby came into the feeble light. When he saw Bobby, he smiled. "Are you lost, my child?"

"Father, I am. I am in great need of somewhere to sleep."

The priest stepped aside and motioned for Bobby to enter.

The inside of the church was rundown and smelled of rotting wood and dust. There was only a rack of small candles lit at the far end just below the altar. Bobby could see the wooden pews, most in disrepair, and faded tapestries on the wall.

"What church is this, Father?"

The priest smiled. "This is the oldest church, still standing, in this town. The Keyport Church of God has been in existence since the early 1800's." He looked at the altar and his smile faded. "Alas, no one worships here anymore, and I'm getting too old to make the proper repairs myself. Some of the artifacts have been stolen over the many years, and I don't even have a likeness of Christ to look at."

Bobby gripped the backpack and looked away. "How do you survive?"

The priest shrugged. "I have my own garden and some of the local boys will run to the store for me from time to time. I also find offerings of food and clothing on my doorstep from anonymous families."

Bobby didn't like the sound of any of his words but couldn't quite put a finger on why it sounded so odd to him. "Why are you still here, if there is no longer a congregation or worshippers?"

The priest smiled. "Two reasons, my child." He started walking down the aisle and Bobby followed. "I've been waiting for a sign, an omen, if you will."

The priest stopped at a door to the right of the altar and pushed it open. "You can sleep here tonight… or what's left of the night, anyway. We'll talk in the morning."

"Father…"

The old man smiled. "Father Ignacio. But you can call me Rocco. Pleasant dreams."

Bobby went to close the door but stopped. "Father, um, Rocco, you said you stayed for two reasons. What was the second?"

"I'm afraid if I leave they'll burn down the church."

* * * * *

Bobby woke to the smell of coffee. Despite his reticence in sleeping in the strange church, he'd fallen quickly to sleep and felt refreshed. Sunlight was streaming through a couple of holes in the ceiling and cracks in the walls.

"Ah, I hope you slept well," the priest said, from the opposite door behind the altar, carrying a steaming ancient coffee pot. "I hope you like your coffee black. I'm afraid I don't have cream or sugar left."

"That will be fine," Bobby said, even though he usually drowned his coffee in both. He watched the priest as he poured two cups and set them on the altar.

"Not very holy of me to use the altar as a table, but I make do." The priest closed his eyes as he sipped the coffee. "It's strong today. I used an extra scoop since I have company."

Bobby felt his stomach growl. "What's the chance we have some bacon and eggs for breakfast, Father?"

"Rocco, please." He lowered his cup. "I'm afraid I don't have much to offer. The bread is mostly stale and I have nothing but water right now."

Bobby took a sip of the bitter coffee and tried not to grimace. "I'll be right back."

The priest looked scared. "No, you can't leave me."

Bobby patted the priest on the shoulder. "It's the least I can do. I'll head back to the diner and buy us some food, unless there's a Publix around?"

"I have no idea what a Publix is."

"Of course not." Bobby again felt like he'd stepped back through time. "I'll be back within the hour."

Rocco looked like he wanted to say more, his eyes darting as his mouth moved, but he simply turned away.

Bobby went outside, into the beautiful late morning sun. As he walked down the main path and through the gate surrounding the church, he looked back and smiled. During daylight hours it looked like any other old church. It needed a new coat of paint and the front steps were sagging, but it gave off a positive vibe to Bobby. He chalked up his wary attitude last night to not getting enough sleep and being on edge.

The walk back to the corner of Broad Street and Route 36 took longer than Bobby thought it would. He strolled down the sidewalks of Keyport alone, although, he was sure, more than once, he felt someone watching him. A quick glance at a home and a curtain fell back into place. A car was slowly coming up behind him just as he reached the diner, but it was an old man in a pickup truck and not the BMW from last night.

But he wasn't getting any real feeling of danger, and that was always a relief. Before entering the diner, he glanced into the parking lot and wasn't surprised to see the Honda Civic still in place.

He went inside and slipped into the same booth as last night since the counter was packed with customers but there were open seats everywhere else.

"Can I help you? Hey, sugar," the same waitress from last night said and smiled. She winked. "Back for more?"

"Do you live here?" Bobby blurted.

She put both hands on the table and sighed. "It sure feels like it. Mandy called out sick so I had to cover her shift. Working a double is no fun, let me tell ya." She straightened up and cocked a hand on her hip. "Is it just the bad coffee you came in for?"

Bobby realized too late what a mistake this was. He should have found a convenience store or somewhere else to get food, because this waitress would always remember him. If shit went down, she'd be more than happy to spill her guts for attention. He should be on his way. Bobby decided to get up and head for the nearest bus station. He reached for his backpack... "Shit."

The waitress looked confused and took a step back. "Forget something?"

"Yes." Bobby rubbed his eyes. He'd left the backpack in the room at the church. *Stupid!* "I need to place an order to go."

"You can do that at the counter."

Bobby didn't want to stand at the counter, and he was hungry. "What if I order food and coffee now and a to-go order at the same time?"

She smiled. "That will work."

He ordered coffee with two extra coffees to go, and a ton of sugar packets and creamers with it. He decided on a sausage and extra cheese omelet with a side of bacon and toast, and another order to take with him. He figured the priest would be sick of vegetables. "How about bagels and cream cheese? Two of those to go, too."

"Be right back with your coffee." As she walked away, Bobby couldn't help but watch her ass as she swung it for him. When she got to the counter, she stopped and turned suddenly, grinning when their eyes met. She caught him and she obviously loved it.

Hell, if he decided to stay an extra day, maybe he could tap that ass. It wasn't like she'd forget him now, anyway. Might as well take advantage. And in the future, if he was gunned down by the police or someone from Black Death, she would be able to brag to all her friends that they had that night. Bobby laughed at his own stupidity and ego, which had gotten him into trouble his entire life.

She came back and poured him some coffee and he noticed the two top buttons on her shirt were now open, giving him a great view as she bent over. "Thinking about dessert?" she whispered.

He openly stared at her chest and smiled. "Yes, I am. Is it too early to place my order?"

She touched his arm. "I hope to get off at four." She leaned close to him. "And I leave here at three."

It took him a second to process what she'd said but when he did he laughed at the innuendo. "I like that."

"You aren't a local. Where are you staying, Hazlet Ramada?"

Bobby was sipping his coffee and feeling good. "I crashed at the church last night, but have no idea where I'll be tonight." He turned to her, thinking his subtle hint would make her smile, but she was moving away from him and shaking her head.

"I'll get your food," she said and averted her eyes as she ran into the kitchen.

What the fuck just happened?

"Looks like you aren't getting laid tonight," the man said as he slid into the booth across from Bobby and put both hands on the table. It was the man from last night at the diner. Bobby was assaulted with the same bad feelings again and struggled to control them.

Bobby picked up the coffee cup and tried to be casual but his hand was shaking.

The man tapped his fingers, obviously enjoying Bobby's discomfort. "How's the coffee?"

Bobby slopped some onto his lips before giving up and putting the cup back down. "Can I help you?" he asked, and was glad his voice didn't crack.

"Yes, you can, as a matter of fact. I like you. Cut to the chase, as they say. It's not hard to see you are a man of action."

Bobby detected a local accent but with some of his words there was a New England slant, like he was born here but spent quite a bit of time up north. Bobby was a master at things like this, detecting inflections, lies as people spoke, as well as their aura.

This guy was bad news, but there was something... different about him, now that he was so close.

Another waitress came up and placed Bobby's breakfast on the table and handed him his to-go bags at the same time.

"Excuse me, waitress? The man needs some more coffee," the man said.

When the waitress hesitated, he stood and walked with her back to the counter.

Bobby dug into his food, trying to calm down. His heart was racing and he wanted to bug out and run until he dropped, but he needed to eat and conserve his energy. He'd been in worse spots than this. He'd stared down the barrel of a loaded gun a few times and been severely wounded. He'd blacked out from pain and was once thrown out of moving speedboat.

As the guy sat back down, Bobby finished his omelet and shoveled the hashbrowns into his mouth.

"Hungry?" the guy asked with a laugh. "Don't worry about the bill. I took care of it for you, and tipped both girls as well. Have you tried the porkroll egg and cheese sandwich yet? It's a Jersey staple."

Bobby wiped his mouth with his napkin before leaning forward. "Who the fuck are you, buddy?"

"Just someone interested in someone hanging around Keyport that isn't a local. They don't usually get too many *tourists*." He smiled. "I'm Harrison Marsh."

"I'm leaving. Nice to meet you." Bobby grabbed his food order and headed for the door. The waitress was staring at him in fear and the entire staff was around her. The diner was quiet, all eyes on him as he pushed through the door and out into the morning sunshine.

He wasn't surprised to see the guy follow him out.

"I didn't catch your name," Harrison said.

"No, you didn't." Bobby kept walking, ignoring the abandoned car as he swept past. He wanted to get his backpack and jump the first bus out of this weird little fishing village.

When the BMW pulled up next to him on the street, Bobby had to laugh. He stopped, made a cursory look to make sure they were alone, put the coffees and bagged food on the curb and pulled his pistol. He leaned into the BMW and pointed it at the guy's head. "Give me a reason why I shouldn't put a fucking bullet in your head."

Instead of cringing in horror, Harrison laughed. "My wife hated when I cursed. She hardly ever did it herself. The last time she did, you know what she said?"

Bobby couldn't believe they were having this casual conversation. "Are you for real?"

"Fuck." Harrison laughed. "She yelled fuck." He dropped his smile. "And then my grandfather dragged her into Keyport Bay to join with the Deep Ones."

"Sorry to hear that."

"I need your help," Harrison said.

"Fuck off. If you follow me, I will shoot you in the face. Do you understand?"

"You are carrying something I need to help me fight them. Is it on you or at the church?"

Bobby almost pulled the trigger. "I will shoot you."

Harrison put his hands up. "Then, on your way, tourist. I won't bother you again. However, I can be found by going to the easternmost end of Walnut Street and following the dirt road south."

"If I see you again, I'll shoot you dead." Bobby leaned out of the car and tucked the pistol in his pants but kept his hand on it. Once the BMW was driving east on Broad Street and he was sure he didn't double back or turn down a side street, he picked up the food and coffee and started to move at a fast clip. He was going to get the fuck out of here and never look back.

* * * * *

Father Rocco was hovering in the doorway when Bobby came up. As soon as he got up the steps, the priest moved back into the darkness of the church and shut the door behind Bobby.

"I brought you some breakfast. And coffee," he said and put the items on the altar before moving into the room he'd slept in. His backpack was where he'd left it and he went to it, putting a hand on the zipper.

"I know why you are here," the priest said from the doorway.

Bobby turned and almost pulled his pistol before relaxing. "You scared me, Father. Don't sneak up on a man like that."

"I'm sorry." The old man's eyes went to the backpack. "I looked. I know what you have, and I know God has sent you."

"There is no God," Bobby said rudely. "I need to leave. Enjoy your food and thank you for letting me crash here."

The priest blocked the doorway with his small body, gripping both sides of the doorway. "I can't let you leave. Not now."

Bobby slid the backpack over his shoulder. "I don't have time for this. I need to be somewhere else."

"Don't you see? They've been able to successfully destroy the holy items over the years. I have nothing to fight them with. Now you show up on my doorstep, with an item of power."

"Life is filled with coincidences." Bobby tapped the backpack. "This is the only thing keeping me alive right now, for whatever reason. I have some very bad men trying to find me because I took this."

"Why did you take it?"

Bobby didn't know. When he thought about it, none of it made sense. Black Death had been contracted by one of their normal shady business partners to retrieve the item from a church in St. Augustine, Florida and bring it to him in Miami. Bones and Tank had gone and lifted it without a problem, but, as soon as Bones had it in his possession, he didn't want to give it up. He wanted to protect it, shield it from evil and run.

So he clubbed Tank as he got on his Harley and didn't stop beating him until he was dead or near dead, and Bones rode north. In Atlanta, he hooked up with an old friend, not connected to the Black Death Motorcycle Club, and he helped Bones with a new identity, as well as a spell to hide him from Laser's scrying powers. So far it had helped. Bobby didn't know how far he needed to run, but he knew it was much farther than this backwater town.

"I don't need to answer you. It doesn't matter. I need to walk out that door and be on my way. Good luck with your problems, Father."

Father Rocco moved out of the way and let Bobby pass. "Please reconsider."

Bobby turned back to him and smiled. "It was actually nice to meet you. I've done some really bad things in my day. I wish we had a few more hours to kill, because I'd love to get in that booth over there and spill my guts. Get this shit off my chest." Instead, he turned and walked back outside into the clear day.

Harrison leaned against his BMW on the sidewalk and waved.

Bobby pulled his pistol and aimed at the bastard.

"Son, put that gun down in the House of God."

"That man is following me."

Father Rocco laughed. "That man is trying to find his missing wife." The priest gently put his hand on the gun and pushed it facing the ground. "What you have in your backpack will help him, don't you see? This is why you're here."

Bobby glanced at the man, who stood with a smile on his face.

"I should shoot him and be done with this."

Father Rocco laughed. "You'll never be done with this until you help us."

"Us?"

"Yes. I've been having dreams about this for a week. It is God's will. We need to help this man find his wife and defeat them."

Bobby closed his eyes as he put the pistol back in his waistband. "Them?" he asked and didn't know why he wasn't walking west down Broad Street and away from this madness.

"The Esoteric Order of Dagon," the man called from the sidewalk. "They took my wife into the bay. I need to get her back."

"How can I help?"

"God will let you know." Father Rocco tapped Bobby on the arm. "I need to get my things. By the time we return, the church will be gone."

Bobby ignored the priest and went to the fence, staring at Harrison. "If this is some bullshit you're pulling over me and the old man, I'll make sure you suffer before you die."

"Not a problem. But you'll see. In the end, you'll understand."

The priest came up with a traveling bag and stopped, turning back to the church and frowning. "This has been my home for innumerable years. I was a small boy when we came here but never fit in." he turned to Bobby. "I'm not one of them, you see. I never will be. Once I walk off this property, they'll sense it and torch the church, like they've been trying to do for decades."

"Then we need to stay and protect it." Bobby opened the gate and motioned for Harrison to come inside.

"I can't enter the grounds," Harrison said and turned to his BMW.

"Why not?"

Father Rocco moved past Bobby and opened the passenger door. "His blood is from here. His family is part of Keyport, even if he wasn't born in this town. He can't enter the church grounds."

* * * * *

The house was ancient. Bobby didn't care to enter, preferring to stand on the front porch with the priest. Harrison didn't bother inviting them inside. He brought lemonade for them, and some cookies on a tray, but the food went untouched as they spoke.

"She was taken two weeks ago." Harrison stared across the great lawn to the water. "It was my grandfather who took her, and not of her own volition." He pointed absently above him. "He was... living in a room upstairs since his death."

"You lost me," Bobby admitted.

Harrison sat down heavily on the top step of the porch. "My grandfather was supposed to have died. That's why Nicole and I came down from Boston. I had the romantic notion of a beautiful old house overlooking the water, someplace nice to raise children, away from the hustle and bustle of the big city."

"Instead, you came to Keyport," the priest said mirthlessly and joined him on the step.

"Someone had padlocked him away. Nicole, for whatever reason, unleashed him. He took her and they met the Esoteric Order of Dagon in the bay. It was storming. I ran across the lawn but she was gone."

"How?" Bobby asked.

"Nicole and my grandfather went into the water together."

"She drowned?" Bobby asked and looked at the serene bay, bathed in sunlight and with seagulls and pleasure boats in sight. It was almost a postcard, but he wondered how different a stormy night would be.

"She is now with them," Father Rocco said. He made the Sign of the Cross and stood. "Her soul is damned, given to the Deep One."

Bobby ignored the cryptic words and walked down the porch steps and through the weeds and small sand hills that made up the lawn. It was actually a nice piece of property. Set off from the road, with a gorgeous view of the Keyport Bay. And all within walking distance of the main thoroughfares, shops, restaurants and bars.

"Anyone know about the guy who runs the bar on Broad Street?" Bobby asked over his shoulder.

Both men had silently joined him on his walk, startling him.

"He is an odd fellow, right?" Harrison asked. "The wife and I went in for some dinner our first night here and he stared at her. Now, I think I know why."

Father Rocco shrugged. "I haven't been off the church property in years. All of these people are strange to me."

"Then why stay?" Harrison asked.

"I felt it was my God-given duty. The one shining light in this den of darkness." He put his eyes down. "And when they sent in non-residents to steal all the religious symbols and kill me, I felt like God had spared me for a greater purpose." He looked at Bobby. "Like you, my son."

"I guess we can't really do anything until tonight. But I'm not going into your spooky house if I can help it. I'm getting some nasty vibes just being on this property. Like the kind you get when you're standing on a desecrated Indian burial ground that's been filled in with violently murdered people, thanks to a serial killer, and then Satan himself decided to build a house on it and live happily ever after."

"I wish it were only Satan," Harrison murmured. "What we're dealing with is closer and infinitely more deadly."

"You two are starting to scare me. It's like you're reading lines from a Boris Karloff movie or something. Enough with the cliché spitting. I need to eat. I'm guessing Dominos won't deliver down to Crazyville."

Harrison laughed. "No, but there is a great Chinese buffet a couple of blocks over. Your treat."

Bobby grinned. "Of course. I'm also in the mood for a drink."

Father Rocco shook his head. "We don't have time for that."

Bobby looked up into the clear sky. "All we have right now is time. You know how these horror movies play out. None of the scary shit happens until it gets dark. I don't want to sit around until midnight and worry about this town attacking me. I need to do some questioning, because that's just who I am."

"Let me lock up," Harrison said.

"Why, afraid someone will break into the creepy house?" Father Rocco said with a laugh. He trailed off as they got into the BMW and pulled back onto Walnut.

They could clearly see the smoke from the fire in the distance, and knew it was the church.

* * * * *

Bobby was going along with something that was beyond him, even with all the paranormal and weird stuff he'd been through in his life. With Black Death, he was part of the team, he knew which side he was on, and he generally knew his role and what to expect.

"I don't even know what this is," Bobby said as he reached into the backpack.

"Not here," Father Rocco said quickly, his eyes skirting around the property. "They are always watching."

Dinner was delicious, and Bobby went to town on the Chinese buffet, filling himself like he'd never done before. When the three men had entered, families and couples hurried with their last plate of food and rushed out. Bobby took it upon himself to pour soda from the fountain for them, since the staff stayed in the kitchen and refused to help. It was quite surreal, like they were lepers.

By the time they'd finished, the sounds of fire trucks were gone and they didn't see smoke in the sky. Father Rocco wanted to go back to the church, but Harrison took him by the arm and led him back into the BMW and home.

Bobby refused to go into the house and the priest concurred. "There is something... off in this dwelling. Something evil resides here," Father Rocco said quietly.

"There are several things residing here," Bobby said with conviction. "My senses are all over the place, even sitting on this porch." Bobby no longer wanted to go to the bar. He wanted to be done with this night and leave.

Harrison dragged one of the living room chairs out for the priest and put it on the porch. "I haven't been back upstairs since Nicole left. I use the bathroom and sleep on a couch with my sneakers on. And I mostly sleep during the day, since it's too spooky at night. At dusk, I come out here and watch the water."

The three men were silent for awhile. As it grew darker, they grew edgier, fiddling with stray twigs, the priest shaking his legs to a fast rhythm, and getting more and more nervous.

"We'll need to go inside and examine the artifact," Father Rocco finally said.

Bobby watched as Harrison and Father Rocco entered the house, but as he stepped to the doorway and moved his foot forward he stopped, repulsed. His gift was in full bloom and his head felt like it was going to explode.

"What's the matter?' Harrison asked.

"I can't go in there," Bobby said, and slumped down into the chair on the porch. He handed his backpack to Harrison and closed his eyes. "Wake me before the fun begins."

* * * * *

It all happened so fast.

Bobby was having a nightmare about a tentacled beast just below the surface of the water when he was violently shaken by Harrison. He instinctively went for his pistol but it was gone.

"Father Rocco went into the painting!"

"What the fuck are you talking about?" Bobby pushed himself off the chair and came awake. He looked around. It was dark out, strange lights over the water. The porch was quiet.

"We don't have time for this. They tried to get the relic from him but he resisted. I was able to pull it from his fingers but he was... sucked into the painting." Harrison hefted the golden item in his hand, which looked like a small staff, only twelve inches long and three inches thick. "We need to get out into the bay and find Nicole."

Bobby shook his head. "We need the priest."

Harrison scoffed. "This isn't about God and the Devil and all of the old man's fairytales. This is real, this is us versus the Old Gods; don't you get it? He is out there and he is gaining power. We need to stop him. But first we need to rescue Nicole. I have a rowboat."

Bobby looked Harrison in the eye. "Where is my weapon?"

"I don't know what you're talking about."

"Bullshit. Hand it over or I will take it from you."

Harrison pointed through the open doorway. "The priest took it with him. He has it."

"He's upstairs?"

"Are you listening to me? He went into the painting. There's no more time left." Harrison ran off the porch and toward the water with the golden staff in hand.

Bobby let him go and steeled himself to ignore the heady feeling, the pain and his primal instincts. He went into the ancient house and walked up the stairs, as if moving through molasses.

Halfway up, even with no lights on, he could clearly see the horrific painting on the wall, taking up several feet of space next to the stairs.

It seemed to move when he didn't look at it closely, and it gave off such a wave of evil that Bobby held onto the railing and began to vomit. When he stopped, only bile spitting from his nostrils and burning his throat, he looked up and forced his will to fight it.

It was a landscape of volcanic fields, angry seas and purple skies. Creatures seemed to shift whenever he looked at another part of the huge mural. Bobby began feeling his mind slip as he held his ground.

When he saw the tiny image of Father Rocco, arms held above him as a large bat-like entity hovered above his head, Bobby tried to reach in and grab the priest.

Lightning seemed to flash and Bobby blinked, his fingers charred as he found himself disoriented and prone at the bottom of the stairs.

Bobby ran from the house and made his way across the lawn to the bay, but Harrison was already just a tiny speck, lights from a multitude of anchored boats behind him.

He needed to get out of Keyport. The BMW was locked and he didn't have the keys, anyway. He started to run. As he reached Broad Street for a straight shot out of town, he saw the procession heading his way.

It seemed like the entire town held torches and chanted, marching toward him.

Bobby cut over a side street and ran right past the charred remains of the church, the smell of burnt wood heavy in the air. His lungs were burning from the running and he stopped to catch his breath.

They came from all directions, moving silently but carrying two by fours, metal pipes and garden tools. Bobby reached for his Ruger LCP 380 ACP but it was still gone.

He fought with his fists until he was driven to the ground and overwhelmed.

* * * * *

Harrison sat on the chair on the porch as the motorcycles roared onto his driveway and parked next to his BMW.

The misty morning was finally dissipating and the feeble sun was trying to break through.

Six burly men got off their bikes and marched forward.

Harrison pulled the Ruger LCP 380 ACP and aimed it at the lead biker. "I would stop right there."

The man laughed. "We're looking for a brother of ours."

"He left."

The man turned to another of his colleagues. "Is it true?"

The man closed his eyes and nodded. "He was here. The object is still here, but Bones is... no longer nearby."

Harrison pulled the golden staff from the chair cushion and tossed it. The head biker caught it with a smile.

"I assume that's what you were looking for? It's useless, you know."

"Where did he go?"

Harrison laughed. "Most likely to the bar on Broad Street. He hangs out there. Ask the bartender; that's who he's been friendly with. You can't miss the place; it's right near the water."

"This place reeks of death. We need to leave," one of the bikers said quietly.

"Thank you for our valuable, and the information." The head biker turned to leave but stopped. "You really should get out more often, dude. You're as white as a ghost."

As they mounted their Harley's and drove off, Harrison put the pistol down on his lap and stared at his arms. He was indeed white, his skin like chalk.

Earlier his hair had fallen out in clumps, white and dead. He pulled his body off the chair and went back inside. He'd need to get into the upper room his grandfather had lived in his last few days and hope the townspeople would lock him inside.

Just like they'd done to his grandfather.

CABAL

Elizabeth Marsh parked in the lot across from the Keyport Fishery and smiled. Seagulls drifted on the slight wind, floating above the fishing boats, looking for scraps. She fought the urge to pull her camera and take a picture of the idyllic scene before her, like something out of a Thomas Kinkade painting. She didn't know any other painters, so he was the go-to name to drop when she was in affluent company.

As a new reporter, trying to rise in the ranks of the Asbury Park Press, she knew the value of knowing as much about everything as possible. She just needed the real life experience, as her editor kept drilling into her.

"You're only twenty-three. At that age I'd already done two tours of 'Nam and seen men die. You need to get out there and find your niche. See what moves you as a reporter, and what people respond to," he'd said over and over. It seemed to be his editor mantra.

"This article will be life-changing," she said with a laugh as she picked up her camera, tape recorder and small notebook. She'd been handed yet another fluff piece: the Broad Street Pub in Keyport was going to be celebrating their 150th anniversary next month. She was assigned to get some interior and exterior shots of the building, interview some locals and the owner, and hand in two thousand words by next Monday.

The smell of the salty air hit her when she got out of the car and she breathed it in. This was America to her: a little fishing village, cradled on the coast of New Jersey, men working with their hands while their wives stayed home and baked bread and chased the kids around.

She walked up West Front Street, admiring the quaint mom and pop shops, so rare these days. While she didn't live in a huge city, Eatontown was big compared to Keyport. A young couple walked past her and she smiled. They put their heads down and cut across the street and away from her.

"Whatever," she mumbled under her breath. She wasn't going to let rude people spoil her time here, and her mind was already trying to picture future stories about Keyport. Maybe she'd get her blog back up and running and ruminate about small town life, with pictures and short essays about it. She liked that. As much as she wanted to be a star at the Asbury Park Press, she thought it would limit her career long-term. She needed to become a multimedia darling, someone who used the technology for her own career moves.

She noticed another two people seeming to move away from her as she turned the corner onto Broad Street. The sidewalk sloped down toward the bay, another block of small stores and the breeze driving a fishy smell at her. It was strong, almost overpowering, and she covered her nose as she quickened her pace.

Luckily the Broad Street Pub was only about halfway down the street; she was nearly jogging when she grasped the door with her free hand and stepped into the establishment.

The door closed behind her, bumping her into the dark bar about a foot. The fish smell was gone, replaced by the strong odor of spilled beer, man-sweat and stale cigar smoke. *It's like I walked onto a pirate movie set*, she thought as she recovered her composure.

Three men sat at the bar, cupping mugs of beer and staring intently at her. The small beaten tables and chairs in the rest of the bar were empty this time of day, and the only lights were above the bar, shining a sickly yellow light across the multitude of liquor bottles standing there, row after row.

Elizabeth took a seat next to one of the men, the youngest (comparatively speaking: he looked to be about twice her age, while the other two looked to be three times) of the bunch, and smiled.

All three gave a silent look before standing in unison and piling into the table farthest away from the bar, almost disappearing in shadow.

"Can I help you?"

Elizabeth turned to see a bald man, with muscular arms and a long graying goatee, standing behind the bar with a dirty rag in hand. He wasn't smiling.

"Are you the owner?"

He shook his head. "Can I get you a drink? Are you lost?"

At the last comment, one of the men in the corner snickered.

Elizabeth wasn't easily rattled, and she put on her best smile. "My name is Elizabeth Marsh, and I'm a reporter for the Asbury Park Press. I'm writing a piece on the upcoming 150th year anniversary of this bar. I was wondering if I could get in touch with the owner, and perhaps speak with you and the staff of the Broad Street Pub?"

When she'd begun talking, his eyes lit up but she kept pressing on, not knowing if he was suddenly interested in what she had to say, or about to toss her out. Since getting out of her car, she'd had nothing but odd experiences in this town.

The young one she'd originally sat next to walked up and slammed his empty mug on the bar next to Elizabeth. "I need another fill, Murph," he said but was staring at her. "What did you say your name was again?"

"Elizabeth." Had he heard of her, maybe read her article about the feral cat problem in Sea Bright in last week's paper?

He shook his head, clearly annoyed. "Your last name."

"Marsh. Why?"

Instead of answering her, he repeated the name to the two men at the table.

The bartender put a cold beer in front of the man but he didn't touch it. Elizabeth thought he suddenly smelled like dead fish but she didn't cover her nose, even though she wanted to. No sense in being rude when she was close to getting some basic information so she could leave.

"Can I get the owner's number or contact information?" she asked the barkeep. She didn't like this place; it gave her the creeps, but she figured she could fake the article by doing some basic online research and going over to the public library.

"They aren't here right now," the bartender said.

"Are you related to Jeb Marsh?" the other man asked her, now leaning in and staring at her face.

"I have no idea. Why, is he the owner?"

The man smiled, rotten teeth shaking in his mouth. "There is a definite family resemblance. Don't you think so, Murph?"

"Yes. I do see it."

Elizabeth had had enough. "Would you mind if I take some photos of the interior for the article?"

The bartender shook his head. "Afraid not. Not without the owner's permission."

"Can I talk to them?"

He smiled, and she knew he was toying with her. "Afraid not."

She left rattled, and was glad to smell the disgusting air rather than spend another minute with that motley crew. Elizabeth took three quick photos of the outside of the bar before jogging back to her car.

* * * * *

Elizabeth waited patiently as the old woman put on her reading glasses, pushing several large reference books off to the side of her cluttered desk.

"What was it you are looking for, dear?" she asked with a smile.

Elizabeth glanced around the small library, which was really just a single room stacked floor to ceiling with books. "I need to do some research and don't see the computer."

"Here is the computer," the old woman said and tapped her head. "It's all stored right here."

Great. This will take forever. "I'm looking for some information about the Broad Street Pub. I was hoping to go through anything you had on microfiche from your archived newspapers."

"We don't archive things like that here, dear."

"So you have no newspapers?"

"I didn't say that." The old woman smiled. "I read and commit them to memory. It goes back to 1962, when I started. Before that my mother was head librarian."

Elizabeth wanted to scream. She thought she could slip into the local branch, copy a few pages from the local paper, and be done. She was better off going back to her office and searching the Asbury Park Press database instead.

"What information do you need about the Broad Street Pub?"

Might as well humor the woman. "With the anniversary coming up, we'll be running an article very soon."

The old woman nodded. "Before it was called the Broad Street Pub, did you know it was called The Murphy Bar? The family still owns it. All told, that spot has been a bar for nearly 250 years, and has been owned by the Murphy family since before the first brick was laid."

"I met the bartender before, but he wouldn't give me any contact information about the owners."

She laughed, a dry raspy sound like crinkling paper. "That's because you met the owner. That would be Dylan Murphy. The first-born son gets the bar and the name." She tapped her forehead with a bony finger. "If my memory serves me correctly, there have been nine owners since the beginning. I do have a great memory."

Elizabeth was annoyed at the shoddy treatment she'd received from him. Even if he didn't care to take part in the article or was embarrassed by the attention, there was no reason to make her look silly. And his cronies didn't help, either. Elizabeth remembered what the other man had asked her. "What information do you have on Jeb Marsh?"

The librarian's eyes clouded over for a second but her smile never faltered. "He owns the only home at the end of Locust Street. Well, he did, anyway. Now his grandson, Harrison, owns the property. Why do you ask?"

"One of the patrons in the bar mentioned his name, since my name is Elizabeth Marsh."

She smiled. "I thought you looked familiar."

"I've never been here."

The old woman stood and walked slowly around her desk. She gripped Elizabeth with her skeletal arms and gave her a hug. "It's so good to see you've returned."

"I've never been here," she repeated more insistently.

The old woman released her. "How is your mother, Eileen? Your father, Jack?"

"How do you know my parents?"

"They were both born here, and so were you."

Elizabeth shook her head. "I was born in Long Branch."

"You were born in the house on Locust Street. As was your father and his brother, Jeb. He was your uncle."

"What happened to Jeb Marsh?"

"He returned to the water. We all return to the bay when our time is up and we receive the Call. Now that you're back in Keyport, you'll see."

* * * * *

Elizabeth was making the turn past Sandy Hook on Route 36 when she decided to call her mother. It rang three times before her answering machine kicked on. And her mother, bless her soul, still used an ancient device for her messages instead of simply using the one that came with phone access. Of course, she still had the bright red rotary phone hanging on the kitchen wall of her tiny apartment in Long Branch.

"Mom, it's me. I have to ask you a question. Call me back when you get this, or I might just stop in. I'm heading into Sea Bright and I can be there in fifteen minutes."

She put the cell phone on the passenger seat and rolled down her window, tasting the fresh ocean air. This wasn't the cloying, deathly scent from Keyport. This was clean, invigorating, and made her happy. She never wanted to live anywhere in the world where an ocean wasn't a quick drive away.

Her phone rang just as she passed into Long Branch, making a left on Chelsea Avenue and parking in a sprawling lot overlooked by condos. "Hey, mom."

"Are you close?"

"I'm in Long Branch already."

"Would it be too much trouble to stop and get me something from the store?"

"Of course not. Bread? Milk? Coffee? Eggs?"

Her mother laughed. "I don't want to put you out. I'll give you the money when you get here. Make sure they give you a receipt this time."

"How about lunch?"

"I couldn't impose."

"Not at all. It gives me an excuse to go to The Windmill and get a hot dog or three."

"And fries?" her mother asked with a chuckle.

"Of course. See you in ten minutes."

* * * * *

Over a quiet lunch, mom and daughter talked about the weather, television shows and other small-talk. Elizabeth finally steered the conversation back around. "Oh, guess what I'm doing a story on? A bar that is 150 years old."

Her mom smiled. "That's interesting. I'm sure you'll knock your editor out of the water with it, as usual."

"It's called the Broad Street Pub."

Her mom just smiled.

"It's an old bar in Keyport."

Her mom's smile wavered for a second before she stood. "That's nice, dear." She began cleaning up the remnants of lunch.

Elizabeth put a hand lightly on her mom's. "We need to talk."

"About what?" her mom asked but refused to look at Elizabeth.

"About Keyport."

"What about?"

Elizabeth could see her mom was trying desperately to keep her composure but it was quite obvious she was troubled. "Where was I born? Where were you and dad born?"

Her mom seemed relieved. "Give me a second and I'll find the birth certificates."

"That's not what I asked." Elizabeth stared at her mom. "I want the truth."

"We got out," her mom whispered, looking around like they were being watched. "We got away from that evil place. Don't go back." Her mom was getting excited now, her eyes frenzied. "Promise me you won't go back there."

"You're confusing me."

"I can't say anything more and neither should you."

Elizabeth was confused. "Why can't you tell me the truth?"

"Even I don't understand the truth, dear. It's for your own good, though. You need to stay out of that town before it consumes you like it did Jeb. It will consume anyone from the family, don't you see? Of course, you don't. Your father and I kept you as far away from Keyport as we could. But Jack was a stubborn man and refused to leave the area."

"Why couldn't he leave?"

"It was the pull of the water. He needed to be close, but not close enough to get sucked back in. Your father used to fish when he was a boy, and he was a fishing boat captain in his twenties."

"I never knew dad fished," Elizabeth said. She was trying to keep her tone casual and keep her mom talking. Her Reporter Mode had kicked in and she was taking mental notes as they moved along in the conversation.

"Not after you were born, though. He decided…" Her mom closed her eyes. "We decided life there wasn't for us anymore, and we got out. Barely."

"Barely?"

"The Marsh family is a prominent one in Keyport, but over the generations other longstanding families have married into us. Grandon, Reynolds, Murphy, and Pike are just some. But don't let the last name alone fool you."

"I won't." Elizabeth had no idea what her mom meant.

"Promise me you won't go back to Keyport. Promise me," her mom said with teary eyes. "I knew we should have moved to the Midwest. I told your father. Somewhere without the ocean. But he wouldn't listen to me. He couldn't help it, you see? He was a Marsh through and through."

Elizabeth didn't push as her mom suddenly stood and began cleaning up the remains of lunch, hustling into the kitchen. All her mom had managed to do was make her more curious about Keyport and her newfound family history in the little sea village.

* * * * *

Locust Street was a dirt road, with gnarled trees pressing in and brushing against the car as Elizabeth crawled down the path. She could picture it being all but impassable if there was a heavy rain or snow.

The trees gave way to a huge, unkempt lawn that fell away to her left and met a slight drop into the bay. You couldn't call what was growing grass. It was more like a blanket of browning weeds, stuck in the sand.

When Elizabeth got out and stared at the ancient house before her, she let out a gasp. Even though it was early morning, she got the eerie feeling the house was alive and pictured what it would look like on a dark, rainy night with lightning bolts shattering just over the roof of the two-story behemoth, thunder breaking over the water.

"You watched too many Hammer Films as a kid," she whispered, but the image remained as she walked up to the porch. She wasn't surprised when the first step squealed under her footstep.

The screen door was ajar, a stray breeze moving it slowly back and forth. Elizabeth raised her hand to knock but hesitated. *Why am I here? To meet some strange relative? To see the place where my dad was born? This made no sense.*

The front door suddenly opened with a loud creaking noise, startling her.

"Can I help you?" the man in the doorway said, rubbing sleep from his eyes. He looked pale, his skin a dull gray and his thin hair filthy and matted to his forehead.

"My name is Elizabeth and I..." she had no idea what to actually say now that she was here. He was actually creeping her out but she couldn't look away.

"Elizabeth what?" He asked.

"What?"

He looked annoyed and rubbed one eye again with a slick hand. "I know you," he said quietly. "At least, I think I do."

"Elizabeth Marsh," she said and wasn't surprised when he immediately came fully awake. His face changed from a look of astonishment, then fear, and then his eyes fell into slits. Like... *a snake*, she thought.

"Who was your father, Miss Marsh?"

She decided this wasn't such a great idea and wanted to run. His mannerisms and his eyes were a bit off...

"My name is Harrison Marsh, and I need you to come inside," the man said as he gripped her wrist with a clammy hand.

Elizabeth went to pull away but his grasp was electric, shocking her into immediate submission as she stumbled into the decrepit house behind him. He paused, still holding onto her, to shut the door, before leading her into the living room and guiding her to the couch.

Harrison sat down across from her, in a plush chair, gazing over the pyramid of rotting pizza boxes on the coffee table. "Would you like something to eat?"

Elizabeth gazed at the cardboard pile.

Harrison chuckled. "I have actual food and drink in the kitchen. I'm afraid I'm not much of a cook. My wife, Nicole, used to do all the household things when she was around."

"I'm sorry to hear that," Elizabeth said. "Did she, uh, pass away?"

Harrison shrugged. "I thought she was alive, but now I'm not so sure."

"I don't understand."

Harrison stood and glanced at the ceiling before putting a finger to his lips. "It isn't safe to talk inside the house. They are up there, listening."

"Who?"

Harrison closed his eyes. "Our relatives, of course."

Elizabeth knew he was right, but she didn't know how it was possible or what it really meant. The familiarity of this dwelling was very strong to her, but she didn't think she'd ever been here. It was more of a presence than an actual memory she was aware of. But she felt as if she'd been in this living room before, years ago, as a child…

There was a subtle thump from upstairs. Both of them jumped.

"What was that?" Elizabeth asked.

"I think someone has returned."

"Your wife?"

Harrison frowned. "I doubt it." He glanced at the stairs leading to the second floor. "At this point, I hope not."

Elizabeth stood.

"Where are you going?"

Her reporter mode was kicking in, and she needed to do something before she was completely freaked out and ran from the house. "I'm going to see who it is."

"You can't go up there," Harrison said and stood to block her. "I won't let you."

"Where is the kitchen?" she asked, trying to throw him off.

"I'll show you," he said and tried to grab her wrist again.

"The next time you put your hands on me you lose a finger. Do you understand?"

Harrison actually smiled pleasantly. "Of course. Forgive me. My nerves are shot at this point. Are you hungry or thirsty?"

"I could use something to drink," she said. Her goal was to follow him toward the kitchen but then dash up the steps. She tried not to show her disappointment when he kept between her and the stairs as they moved, watching her every step.

The kitchen was filthy. The appliances were old and antiquated, and everything was covered in a sheen of dust or dirt, obvious animal droppings littering the four corners. The kitchen table was overflowing with more pizza boxes, empty plastic two-liter soda bottles and old books.

"The maid is on vacation this week," Harrison said. He dumped a tall stack of loose papers off one of the kitchen chairs. "Please, sit."

Elizabeth made to drop down onto the chair when she spotted the closed door on the other side of the kitchen. With any luck, it led to stairs going up. Without another thought, and as Harrison turned to the grease-streaked refrigerator, she made a dash for the door.

It swung open into darkness.

"Don't go down there!" he shrieked.

Too late, she took the steps two at a time and plunged into the pitch black.

* * * * *

What are you doing? Elizabeth thought as she stumbled off the last step and nearly twisted her ankle. She felt around for a light switch but there wasn't one when her fingers brushed against the wall.

She looked back up the steps, but it was dark. *Did he close the door behind me?* She was expecting him to be up there, sunlight behind his head, screaming for her return. There was only an eerie silence and a wet earthy smell. Now she was trapped.

The ground felt spongy beneath her feet, like mud or loam. Elizabeth took a tentative step forward and then another. She could sense a vast space all around her as she slowly moved. She snapped her fingers and heard the echo.

A flashlight or lantern would be a nice addition right about now, she thought. Elizabeth took another step before she had one of those face-palm moments.

"My cell phone!" she said, pulling it from her pocket. She turned it on and grinned at her ingenuity.

There were many red, angry eyes shining back at her in the small area the feeble light penetrated...

But she didn't have time to think about them because her panicked next step didn't hit solid ground, or even squishy ground. It hit nothing, and she toppled forward into a dark pit.

* * * * *

Her cell phone was buzzing on vibrate next to her head and it sounded like angry bees trying to crawl into her ear. The faint light was on for a second as her eyes struggled to adjust, but then all went black again.

Elizabeth wasn't afraid of the dark as a child, but this was absolute black. She couldn't see her hand in front of her face. She felt around on the dirt floor until she found her phone and was comforted by the soft glow of the screen.

As her eyes adjusted again, she spun around slowly and took in the chamber she was trapped in. There were no tunnels or exits except one, set about ten feet above her. She couldn't see the ceiling with the light.

When she completed her full circle, she gasped. Directly behind her, seated against the wall, were two men and a woman.

One of them, obviously a priest by his dress, smiled through cracked lips. He was old but looked positively ancient. Emaciated. "Don't be alarmed. We are the few good people you will meet down here."

"Where are we?"

"Hell," the gruff biker-looking man, next to the priest, said. He didn't stand but offered a hand. "I'm Bones and this here is Father Rocco." When Elizabeth didn't take his hand, he pointed a meaty thumb at the woman lying near them in the fetal position. "She's Nicole. I imagine, if you came in through the house, you've met her crazy sonofabitch husband. He doesn't even realize she's with us."

Elizabeth's head hurt and she leaned against the wall. The reporter in her was trying to process the data but her emotions were getting in the way. She wanted to cry.

"Are you injured?" Rocco asked her.

"No." She patted herself down, but knew nothing was broken. "Not a scratch." She looked up. "How far of a drop is it?"

Bones shrugged and stood. "No clue. I was attacked by the townspeople and knocked out. When I came to, I was here."

Elizabeth looked at Rocco.

"I got sucked into a painting."

Elizabeth waited for the punch-line but Father Rocco wasn't laughing. "Should I even ask?"

"Probably not. I don't understand it myself. This house... this entire town, is under the grip of immense evil. The Esoteric Order of Dagon has sunk its fangs into the good citizens of Keyport, it would seem."

"That's being a bit dramatic, Rocco. I seriously doubt there were ever any good citizens of Keyport. These in-bred monsters have been doing this for eons. Who knows how many others have been trapped down here?"

Elizabeth used her cell phone glow to look at the only exit from the cavern: the natural-hewn hole. "Why don't we just go through there?"

Nicole whimpered.

"*They* live through there," Father Rocco said quietly.

"Who?"

"You mean *what*," Bones said. "They are like blind vicious dogs, with rat heads and... weird tentacles."

"Hell Hounds," Rocco said.

"Here we go with the dramatics again. Not everything has a religious connotation," Bones said. "They are just really fucked up monsters that get pissed when we try to get into the hole."

"How high up is the way I came in?"

"No clue." Bones pointed at Nicole again. "She has been useless since we got here. I'm not sure what her deal is. I'm guessing she's in shock. And she smells like she went swimming in the bay."

"She did. She was abducted by the Order and rowed out as a sacrifice," Rocco said.

"She doesn't look bad for a sacrifice. Usually, it entails being killed." Elizabeth held the cell phone as high as she could but she couldn't see the ceiling.

"Conserve your battery," Bones said.

"Now what?" Elizabeth asked.

"We wait for God to save us," Father Rocco said.

Bones snorted and Elizabeth turned the cell phone off, plunging them back into ultimate darkness.

* * * * *

Elizabeth must have been sleeping because her neck hurt and her senses came alive. Had she heard something? She was slumped against the wall.

"Keep the light off. Trust me," Bones suddenly whispered in her ear, startling her. "I think one of the, uh, Hell Hounds is down here with us."

She could hear the shuffling but couldn't gauge where the thing was. It was breathing heavily and maybe sniffing.

"They might be blind. Don't move," he said again in her ear. "The last time they came down, they sniffed us but no one got bitten."

Elizabeth wondered if he said it to make her feel better, or was just stating a fact. Either way, she was now freaked out. Even more than before, if it that was possible.

And the thing was coming up to her. She smelled it and it repulsed her. It stank of putrid sea water and dead fish. She had the image Bones had told her running through her mind, playing tricks with the dark before her. Could she see or hear the tentacles, or was it her mind playing tricks?

Elizabeth wanted to stand but it was suddenly right there, sniffing her face from inches away. The breath was as bad as the stench coming off the body, and she swallowed bile, refusing to make a noise.

Her stomach lurched. *Do not throw up*, she tried to will herself. *Do not puke.*

It burned up her throat and she spewed the contents of her lunch she'd had with her mom, some of it splashing back off the beast.

Elizabeth rolled to her right, puking again, as she raised her cell phone, defensively, and turned it back on.

The beast was blinded, its red eyes pulsing as it began to scream in pain. *They can see*, she thought stupidly. *I blinded it.* The creature was the stuff of nightmares, and just as Bones described but so much more hideous. Elizabeth convulsed again but there was nothing left to release.

Bones drove a biker boot into the thing's head. "Keep the light on it," he shouted.

She did as she was told, watching in fascination as Bones kicked and pummeled the creature, which was no taller than a German Shepard. The tentacles shimmered and danced but didn't seem to be attacking Bones as he drove it into the ground with each stomp.

Father Rocco was praying to God about forgiveness and killing one of His creatures, but Elizabeth knew beyond a shadow of a doubt this vile abomination wasn't created by God.

When the creature stopped moving, Bones kicked it one last time. He was breathing heavily. "We need to get out of here before his friends show up."

"How?"

"Up. The three of us can see how far it is to the top. It can't be that bad since you didn't break anything when you fell." Bones went to the side and planted is feet, putting his hands on the wall. "Climb up, and do it quickly. Father, you're first."

"What about Nicole?" Elizabeth asked.

"Nicole, can you hear me?" Bones didn't move from his spot but yelled to her, still wrapped up in herself.

"I won't leave without her," Elizabeth said with conviction.

"Then we stay here and die with her," Bones said. "Or we get the fuck out of here and get some help. She isn't going anywhere, look at her. Would you sacrifice all four of us for her?"

"Fine." Elizabeth turned to the priest. "Get up there before I think too much about this."

Father Rocco didn't waste time, climbing onto Bones and standing on his shoulders. "I think I can reach the lip of the crater if I stretch," he said excitedly. "But, without a third person, we'll never get out."

Elizabeth stood behind Bones and readied herself for the dash up the two men when she heard the growl from the tunnel behind her.

Only it wasn't a growl as much as a wet, slobbering barking noise, as if the monster was drowning.

"Let's get moving, ma'am," Bones said. "I can't protect us if we're still trying to climb out. Move that little ass of yours."

Elizabeth smiled despite the situation, knowing she was insane. *Little ass of yours? I like that*, she thought. *If I ever get out of this shit-hole alive, I'm going to eat better, and go back to the gym, and live each day to the fullest. And get a new job.*

She got up and over Bones with ease, since he was so much bigger than her. Once she gripped Father Rocco, however, she felt the man as if he were a sparrow. There was no way she was going to climb up and over him without breaking his ribs or knocking him to the ground.

"Here they come," Bones said.

Elizabeth put her hands on the priest's shoulders and her knee into his back, pushing him against the wall. He grunted but didn't complain. She pulled herself up, at the same time pushing down on him. He wobbled but held steady.

"Can you feel the cellar floor?" Father Rocco said through clenched teeth.

Elizabeth stretched as she managed to get her knees onto his bony shoulders. Her hands went up until the wall disappeared. "I think I did it," she said and tried to grip the floor.

But it was dirt, and she only managed to pull some gravel down on top of them.

"I can't get it."

"Stand up on me," Father Rocco said.

"Do something," Bones yelled. "You're getting heavy and they are sniffing my privates right now."

Elizabeth stood, using the wall as a brace and trying to keep the bulk of her weight off the priest. She knew instinctively, even in complete darkness, she was above the floor and felt the dusty air on her face. She planted her hands and pulled herself up and over, onto the floor.

"I'm up," she said. "Give me your hand."

Father Rocco grabbed her and she tried to pull him up, but despite his size, he was still too heavy for her to do it alone.

"I can't hold this pose for long," Bones said.

"I can't get a good grip and pull him up." Elizabeth sighed in frustration. They were so close to escape.

Father Rocco released his grip from her. "Go find some rope, or some help. We're wasting time."

Before she could reply, he let go, and she could hear him climbing back into the hole in the dark.

"Are you sure?" she asked.

"Hurry," Bones said. "They are all around us."

Elizabeth stood up and turned the cell phone back on, hoping to find something in the cellar of the ancient house to rescue them.

The red eyes were all around her. The first Hell Hound stepped into her cell phone light and bared its insanely sharp teeth.

* * * * *

Bones tried to rub feeling back into his shoulders. Even as light as Father Rocco was, it was still a strain to keep him aloft. The demonic dogs were growling low in their throats, as if making sure Bones and the priest knew where the limit was for them to move.

They are keeping us herded against the wall, Bones thought. *These aren't stupid animals.* He decided to test the theory while they waited for Elizabeth to return with either a rope or the police.

Two steps forward and he could feel the beast snap powerful jaws near his crotch. Bones jumped back, slamming against the wall.

"I don't think we're allowed to move," Father Rocco said. "I vote we stay still and wait for her return."

"I am going to agree," Bones said. He didn't know how long before the beasts would attack them.

And that was when Elizabeth suddenly returned... or part of her.

Her severed arm, still clutching the lit cell phone, dropped into the center of the pit. It cast a beam of light on the two men, who both visibly slumped.

Father Rocco threw up and Nicole moaned softly behind the monsters.

The dozen Hell Hounds, fiery eyes caught in the glow, barked in unison and advanced on the two men.

DAGON

Matthew DiNardo didn't know which was sweating more in this oppressive heat: the glass of lemonade sitting on the kitchen table, or he with the thick ill-fitting suit jacket.

"My little girl will be down in a minute," the Minister Cecil said, dropping his six and a half foot frame into a protesting chair across from Matthew. His hand hid his own glass of lemonade. His emphasis had been on the words "little girl," and Matthew put his hands in his lap so the imposing man couldn't see them shaking.

Matthew could only nod and smile, but the movements felt awkward like he'd never done them before. The minister was smiling at him but, behind the smile, he knew a million horrible questions were spinning through his head. A barrage of questions Matthew didn't want to answer was percolating. He could see it behind the man's eyes. He glanced at the stairs leading up to Tina's room. Somewhere, up above, she was getting dressed. Maybe she was in her panties and bra right now.

Minister Cecil cleared his throat and Matthew nearly knocked over the lemonade when he jumped. The minister smiled again but now Matthew noticed there was no warmth behind it, only probing questions.

"What do you do for a living, son?"

Matthew couldn't smile. He couldn't produce spit in his dry mouth. "I'm an author," he managed to squeak out. He hoped her father didn't notice the hitch in his voice.

"Interesting," the minister said, and Matthew knew it wasn't just a simple statement. The man had made his decision about the boy and the verdict would soon be in. Matthew glanced at the stairs again, wondering if he'd be leaving with Tina for this date. If he was a gambling man, he'd give himself no better than three-to-one odds.

"What do you actually write?"

Ten-to-one odds, Matthew thought. "I write horror stories."

"Fiction?" the minister asked with a dismissive grunt and, suddenly, became interested in his own sweating lemonade glass.

Matthew wanted to get up and run out the front door, down the path and dive into his car and never look back. This was going even worse than he had imagined. When he'd asked Tina out two months ago, he knew at some point he'd have to meet her parents. Since her mother was out of town and he'd kept putting it off, he thought this would be the perfect time. Now he knew why Tina was so hesitant to have him meet her father. *Her minister father*, he thought. *This is such a nightmare.* He knew now the mother was the buffer between father and daughter, and he'd played the wrong hand and lost.

"Do you write as well as Stephen King?" her father quickly asked, staring, once again, at Matthew.

"I wish," he said with a laugh, hoping the old man would join him in a snicker. He didn't.

"I think King is a poor writer, with too much gratuitous sex and violence in his work. He's no Faulkner and couldn't hold a candle to some of the great Christian writers, either classic or contemporary."

"Hmm… interesting," Matthew finally said when it was obvious the man was looking for some sort of answer. Matthew had no idea who Faulkner was, and he was sure he'd never read anything labeled Christian fiction. He didn't even know it was a real thing. Maybe, if he wanted to keep seeing Tina, he'd have to read a bit and suck up to the old man.

"What are some of the inspirational classics you take note of?"

"I'm a big fan of the newer guys, I guess you could say. Keene, Everson, McKinney, Clegg… Edward Lee and Carlton Mellick."

"Never heard of one of them."

"I also grew up reading H.P. Lovecraft," Matthew added with a smile, which dropped when the minister looked like he'd sucked on fifty lemons at once.

A large finger was aimed at Matthew's face. "Not only was the man a bigoted racist, but he wasn't a very good writer. Anyone who creates and puts so much effort into trying to defame God with his own set of pathetic creatures will not be mentioned in my home. He was a charlatan and a fraud, and his Dark Gods or Greater Gods or whatever he created was an abomination."

"That's kinda the point," Matthew said defensively.

The minister was red-faced and looked like he was about to explode. He turned away from Matthew and glared up the steps. "Darn, Tina, this young man is down here waiting for you. Slap on some clothes and get yourself together."

* * * * *

Sorry it took so long," Tina said when they got to his Kia Spectra. He opened the door for her, not because he was a gentleman but because the brackets had rusted out and if you swung the door too far, it was liable to fly off the car.

"Not a problem, your dad and I had a lovely conversation," he said through gritted teeth. They'd sat in silence another six minutes until she'd finally come downstairs. Matthew wanted to ask what the heck took so long, since she was wearing a pair of faded blue jeans and a boring red top. Her hair was back in a ponytail and she didn't have any makeup on, which drove him nuts. She needed to look her best when they went out. What if someone he used to date was around and saw this Plain Jane he was dating now? He'd dated strippers, for God sakes.

OK, he never really dated one, but he'd once given a stripper named Jasmine a ride home when her Porsche had broken down. She'd complained his car smelled like cabbage, and she would avoid him in the strip-club whenever he came in. But he'd twisted the story a bit for his friends (he was a writer) and voila! He had his stripper-banging story.

Tina didn't get into the car. "Did he ask you about your faith?"

"He was too busy asking me about my job."

"What did he say when you told him you were unemployed?"

Matthew wanted to scream. "We've been over this a million times. I have a job. I'm a writer."

"You haven't sold a single story in weeks. You said so yourself. A job means you make money doing it." Tina looked down at her feet. "Just saying."

"You sound like my old man now. I told you: this is going to work out, and I'll have more money than I know what to do with. Just have patience." Matthew smiled. "You know I really like you, right?"

Tina smiled and kissed him on the cheek.

"You know I love you," he whispered.

"I told you to stop saying that," Tina said and got into the car.

Matthew grinned as he walked around the car to the driver's side. He'd said he loved her on their third date and it shook her. He really did think he loved her, because she was a great gal. Tina was the first chick he'd dated who hadn't put out, in the backseat of his car or in a shitty motel room in Sayreville, on the first or second date. Usually, the first. These Hazlet bitches were easy. Like shooting chubby fish in a barrel.

Tina was a pretty girl. She was a little on the plump side but he liked her curves. Best of all, she was very self-conscious about her weight and he would make subtle jabs at her, when they ate out, to keep her in check.

"Wow, another cookie? You really like those," he said the other night when they were at his parent's house and she'd eaten two Oreo cookies. It worked another way, since the cookies were actually his mom's and, if she found out he had a girl in the house or she was eating her snacks, she'd be pissed. Even in his mid-twenties, he had to follow his parent's rules if he wanted to live in their dining room.

Matthew slid into the car and started it, doing his best to ignore the loud squeal of the belt as it started. After twenty seconds, the car relaxed a bit, and only the cracked dashboard made noise as it rumbled with the engine. "Where do you want to eat tonight?"

Tina shrugged. "I don't care." She never had an opinion. If he was paying, it would be Keyport Diner or a fast food place. If Tina offered, they could go to a nice seafood restaurant in Sea Bright or to a chic café in Red Bank.

Matthew made a big show of pulling out his wallet and checking his funds before pulling away from her house. "I'm a little short tonight. I have to buy stuff for, um, my writing. A new printer ink and some stamps and things."

Tina looked back at her house. "I could go inside and ask my father for some money."

Screw that. The old man already hates me. "How does the diner sound?"

"I don't care."

Matthew smiled. "Keyport Diner, here we come." He glanced back at her house when he pulled away from the curb and saw her father standing, with his massive arms folded, and watching them.

* * * * *

Father Rocco woke with a start, spitting out dirt and gravel from his dry throat. He tried to rise but there was something over him. He panicked. *Am I dead? Buried alive? In Purgatory?*

He realized, with relief, he was in a dumpster. Covered with a cardboard box. But why? He remembered the pit and the evil hounds and... the people he was in the hole with. Had Bones and Nichole escaped as well? Rocco didn't know how he'd gotten here, or where *here* actually was. He instinctively knew he was still in Keyport, though. He knew beyond a shadow of a doubt he would spend his last minutes in this godforsaken town.

He was surprised to see he was in the alley behind the Broad Street Bar & Grille. Had he been tossed out the back door of the establishment? He doubted it. There was something evil about the bar, he was sure. It was situated right in the center of the small downtown area, on the main street leading through town and to the docks. The bar's owner was also someone to be feared. Everyone in town knew it, but no one knew exactly why. Dylan Murphy was the ninth of the Murphy brood to own the place in the 150 years it had been situated on Broad Street. He was quite easily the meanest of the bunch if you weren't a local or didn't follow his agenda, and now it was all becoming clear to Father Rocco. He was more than a bartender and business owner in Keyport. He was the puppet master behind all the goings-on. Father Rocco glanced at the sky and prayed God was going to give him the strength he'd need to fight the good fight.

Father Rocco knew there would be no help coming his way. He was on his own, a crumbling old man without a church but with his strong faith intact. Because of the evil in Keyport, his devotion had grown stronger. It was no coincidence the Good Lord had made sure he was still inside the city limits. Rocco felt the intensity and foreboding brewing in town. There was something mesmerizing going on, and it would need to be stopped very soon.

"God, grant me the power to succeed as I face my unearthly foes," he intoned with a whisper. He stepped out onto Broad Street, expecting to be attacked at any moment. Instead, the street was preternaturally quiet, as if the town was holding its breath. Without his church and home, he had nowhere to go as a safe haven. It had been burned to the ground days ago. Or had it been weeks? So many things had transpired in such a short time, and he had no idea how long he'd been held captive.

He lifted his hands, dirty and calloused. He smelled like the earth. Rocco couldn't remember when he'd ever been filthier, and he didn't like it. He felt beaten, a broken old man facing such a monumental task. He only had his faith. Was it enough this time?

"I know I don't deserve to ask you, Oh Lord, but I need some strength to go along with my conviction now. I need some help in the coming battle to be waged. I ask you to look down on me. Give me a sign."

A rusting Kia Spectra went past on West Front Street and the kind face of a God-fearing child peered out at him. Their eyes met and Father Rocco could see the life behind them. He knew what it meant. With a smile, he looked to the sky and spread his hands. "Thank you, Lord."

He began walking, as quickly as his old bones would let him, grateful when he saw the tail lights glow red as the car slowed, across from Keyport Fishery, and pull into the lot near the dock.

* * * * *

"Why are we here?" Tina asked, as Matthew pulled into the empty lot and killed the engine. "I have to be home soon. You know my father will be displeased if I'm even a minute late."

"Displeased? I like that. I would have said pissed, but I know you don't use words like that," Matthew said.

"Those words are disrespectful." Tina didn't like all the profanity Matthew used around her, especially when other people were within earshot. He also used the Lord's name in vain, and she had lost track of the number of times he used sexually charged expressions or called people curse words, especially when he was driving. She often thought about what she was doing dating him, and, when she was alone, she was sure the next time he picked her up she was going to break it off and move on.

But Tina had nothing to move on to. She had no options when it came to men, and she knew it. While her family often fawned over her hair and her smile, she knew men didn't really find her frumpy outfits and lack of makeup exciting in this day and age. She didn't even own a makeup case, and had never had cause, before Matthew, to try to look pretty. She knew she was failing at it, anyway.

"You know I'm just playing. Lighten up, babe. If I didn't really love you, I wouldn't be me around you. Good and bad and all that jazz, you know. We need to be open and honest with each other. How else are we going to spend the rest of our lives together?"

Tina thought he was moving way too fast, but she wasn't one for confrontation. She knew her father would never give her an ultimatum, but, this afternoon, when Tina had mentioned Matthew was going to take her out on another date, her father had decided to meet this boy. Feel him out, and see what his plans in life were. If he had any. There was also an underlying, unspoken thought: why would he be interested in Tina?

"The rest of our lives? We haven't been dating long enough for big plans."

Mathew laughed and tapped on the steering wheel with his fingers. He was always a ball of nervous energy, his hands or legs in motion. He hummed and sang along to songs in his head and Tina tried to ignore them, especially the songs he sang about sexual encounters and violent imagery.

"All I have is big plans, and you're going to be my Angel Girl, and we're going to be rich and famous together."

"Doing what?"

Matthew moved suddenly, leaning into her and putting his face close to hers. She thought he was going to kiss her, but instead he grinned. "Doing anything and everything, don't you get it? Once my writing career swings into high gear, we can travel the world. Haven't you ever wanted to see Paris?"

"Not really. I like it in New Jersey. I don't need to travel."

Matthew scoffed. "There's nothing here to like. It's smelly and dirty and crowded, and people are arrogant jerks. I'm talking about culture and foreign languages and strong beer. I can't write about the world unless I see it."

"You write stories about folks doing horrible things to each other." Tina had read a couple of his short stories and they were appalling, especially the zombie ones. People getting ripped apart and doing bad things to one another, without compassion. Matthew had gotten mad when she said she didn't want to read any more of them because they were too cruel and violent. One of the stories even had a young boy who killed neighborhood cats and dogs. Who wanted to read about stuff so evil?

"I write stories that make people think, even the simpletons from Jersey. What good is high literature if it doesn't move you in some way? Stephen King and jokers like him are so tame in today's climate of horror writing. I'm the new line of extreme horror, and I make people stand up and take notice."

Tina was about to ask what he was talking about, since she knew it had been weeks since his last sale. His self-published stories were routinely given bad reviews for grammar and story errors. He'd be mad if he knew she went online and read them, but she wanted to know if everyone had the same opinion of his writing as he did. Most people did not.

"I support you in your career," Tina said. "But I'd rather not read it. Some of the anti-religious titles you have really bother me."

"Like what?"

"Something about Jesus," she said quietly. If her father found out some of the crazy things Matthew wrote, she'd never be allowed to date him. Again, she wondered if it was a bad thing.

Matthew laughed. "Ah, you are talking about my story in the cannibal anthology, *Zombie Christ*. What a classic."

"That is a horrible title."

"Wait until you read it. It's about this deranged guy who thinks everyone is a zombie, and he has to kill the new Jesus, like the Anti-Christ, before he is birthed into this world."

"Please stop talking about it," Tina said and put her hands over her ears. "I don't want to know."

Matthew didn't seem to be listening to her, rambling on about killing and cooking victims and the smell of human flesh sizzling on the grill.

Finally, Tina had enough. She opened the car door and leapt out.

"Wait, where are you going?" Matthew asked.

"Home," she said, just before crashing into the priest as he came shuffling to the car.

* * * * *

Dylan Murphy stood on the weed-riddled lawn and watched as two men launched the small boat with its captive contents. "Let's try this again," he said to the group behind him. He turned to Harrison. "Without any more problems."

"It wasn't my fault." Harrison looked away, back at his grandfather's house he'd inherited. He'd left the upper bedroom light on again. Or maybe someone else had. He shuddered. This wasn't what he had in mind when he came back to New Jersey. He wanted a peaceful new beginning for Nichole and his life, maybe a baby and new friends and a reconnection with his past. He didn't foresee this ancient house smothering him, a barren life where they should have seen happiness in a small town, the cabal that was Keyport, the Esoteric Order of Dagon taking over his life, and the rampant evil forces.

"So emotional. Did I say it was your fault? I merely pointed out things could have been done differently. Stop being such a baby. There is much work to do tonight," Dylan said.

"Why does it have to be my wife?" Harrison asked, aware he might get attacked for the open rebelliousness of the question.

He was surprised to see Dylan smile. "We do not choose the outlets. We simply do as we are told by Him." Dylan pointed at the slowly moving rowboat. "This time the sacrifice will go on without incident. Those to the north will never laugh at us again, for we do not sit silently and wait for Cthulhu to wake eons from now. We help him to see we are no longer interested in toiling away while he sleeps. We need him to rise before it is too late."

"You are quite mad," Harrison said quietly.

Dylan looked at the group around him, some carrying torches. "Did you do what was foreseen?"

"Yes," one of the older men said. "The priest and the biker have been set free."

"What? Why?" Harrison asked, fear gripping him. "They'll kill me if they find me."

Dylan shrugged. "Then I suggest you don't get found. Cthulhu has spoken, and they are no longer important to us. I will not have senseless bloodshed, so we released them."

"What if they go to the authorities?"

"How can they? I said they were let go from the pit. I did not say they could escape Keyport. I've made arrangements. No one will be leaving tonight. We're taking out the bridge leading north, closing the roads to Route 36 with a massive sewer break, and the Esoteric Order of Dagon will be patrolling for those who need to be inside on this glorious night. I suggest you go back to the house and await the final command."

"This is madness," Harrison said as he stomped away, trying not to look back as his wife was, once again, led to her doom in a rowboat.

* * * * *

Matthew was pissed. Not only had Tina acted like a bitch and gotten out of the car, but now this twisted old man was harassing her. "How about you walk away and leave her alone?"

The old man ignored him, which made Matthew angrier. This guy was going to run interference between Matthew and Tina, and he couldn't have it. He needed her mad at him so the makeup make-out session that followed would be intense. He'd tell her he loved her again and he was sorry for being so rude or whatever she wanted to hear, and then he'd see how far he could get with her in the backseat of his car. But this guy was in his way.

"I won't tell you again," Matthew said and tried to get between the man and Tina, who was leaning against the back of his car and hugging herself. "I will fight an old man."

"Matthew, please. Father Rocco needs my help," Tina said.

"I'm not helping this smelly old dude. Did you take a bath in garbage?"

The old man smiled. "I woke up in a dumpster. I apologize for my ripeness but there is really no time to clean up. Time is not on our side tonight, I fear." He turned back to Tina. "We must act quickly."

"Tell me what needs to be done," Tina said.

"What are you talking about?" Matthew put an arm on Tina's shoulder. "I'm sorry for telling you about my story. I'll take you home so your dad doesn't freak out."

Tina shook her head. "I need to stay here, in Keyport, and help Father Rocco."

"What, is he from your church or something? One of your dad's Baptist buddies?"

"Your father is a minister?" Rocco said and grinned. He looked up. "This is truly the sign I needed." He turned back to Tina. "We have much work to do. Where do you live?"

"In Hazlet."

Rocco stopped smiling. "We won't make it out of Keyport. I was hoping your dad could help me as well. But beggars can't be choosers, as they say."

Matthew shook his car keys. "I'm leaving."

The priest and his date were talking about bullshit like heaven and hell and other nonsense, so he got into the car and started it. He glanced in the rearview mirror but they hadn't noticed and Tina was still against the trunk. What the hell? Matthew was hoping she'd get his subtle hint and get in the car, but she was too busy with the old man, who was probably a pedophile. Matthew was so going to put this jerk into his next story and kill him off in the most horrible way.

"I am driving away," Matthew said as he got back out and left the car running. "Unless you're planning to sit on the trunk while I drive, I suggest you move... or, better yet, get in the car."

"Sorry," Tina mumbled before stepping away from the car and following the priest a few feet away.

"I don't want to see you anymore," Matthew said loudly.

Tina and the priest were still talking, and the old man was saying weird words that sounded made-up.

Matthew got back in the car and drove away, watching them in his mirrors as he drove past Keyport Fishery and headed north. She'd be calling him in the morning and begging for forgiveness, and he'd use it to his advantage. Tina would be on her knees by tomorrow night, asking for him to unzip his fly and…

"What the hell now?"

The road just over the bridge was blocked off, orange drums and flashing lights and a sign announcing the road was closed. They'd come this way not thirty minutes ago. Matthew couldn't see anything wrong with the road ahead.

He got out of his car and looked around, but he didn't see anyone or anything, besides the blockade, to keep him from driving over the bridge. He didn't have time for this shit.

Matthew had grabbed the first work horse in his way and started dragging it off to the side when he saw a shadow detach from the other side of the road. A flash of light showed a weathered face as a man lit his cigarette with a match.

"I wouldn't do that if I were you," the man said. "In fact, I'd put it back where you found it, turn your piece of shit car right around, head back into town and go find a nice place to hide for the evening."

"Why would I do that?" Matthew said, trying to sound confident.

The man stepped into the light and smiled through cracked and yellowed teeth. "Because things are about to get interesting around here, and everyone should stick around and be a part of it… just in case we need some warm bodies."

Matthew ran and got back into his car, locking the door. He toyed with the idea of simply crashing through the barrier. It would only add a couple of new dents to the Kia, so it was no big deal. He thought, if he backed up and stomped on the gas, he could get enough momentum to bust through and maybe knock over the barrels, or there might be enough space to get around them.

The man knocked on the window, startling Matthew. "I wouldn't do that if I were you. Put it in reverse, make a K-turn, and get back into town." The man pulled up his shirt, revealing a handgun tucked into his waistband. "I'm not playing, boy."

Matthew decided it would be in his best interest to go back to the parking lot and find out what Tina and the priest were planning.

* * * * *

The parking lot across from the Keyport Fishery was empty by the time Matthew pulled back in and parked in the same spot as before. He got out and looked around. Nothing. It was quiet. He wanted to call out to Tina but decided against it because... well, because he was scared. The man at the blockade had freaked him out, and he kept looking over his shoulder and expecting him to come walking up any second. Matthew decided to search quietly for Tina. How far could the old priest walk?

The docks were, to Matthew, the obvious place to look first. He walked along the weathered boards, past silent fishing boats, but there was no one around. The cool breeze, off the bay, made him shiver.

"Hello?" he finally called out, afraid someone or something would answer him back. Something splashed in the water just beyond the closest fishing boat. It was dark and he wouldn't have been surprised if a thick fog rolled off the water and shadowy figures with glowing red eyes came at him.

"Calm down," he murmured, scaring himself. This wasn't a stupid horror movie. He didn't have to be freaked out, because bad stuff like that only happened in the movies. And in bad horror books. Not the ones Matthew wrote.

He pulled out his cell phone and laughed when he saw he had five bars. In every movie he saw, the phone was dead or he couldn't get a strong enough signal. He called Tina and was relieved when he heard the first ring.

There was another three rings before her voicemail clicked on. "Tina? Where are you? Call me back."

Another splash in the water, this one closer and louder, startled Matthew. He began walking away, crossing the tight street and getting as far from the water as he could.

Matthew looked back and nearly wet himself. Something was pulling itself from the water and climbing onto the docks.

* * * * *

"This was my church and my home for many years, until the town was overrun by this nightmare," Father Rocco said. He leaned heavily against the charred gate surrounding his former haven. "I kept my mouth shut when they came and threatened me. I thought God would take care of them. I was arrogant and did not see He was trying to tell me to do something with His power. I hid behind my shrinking congregation and my own beliefs. I should have acted years ago."

"You had no idea," Tina said after a moment. She was shaking.

"Oh, but I did." Father Rocco stabbed the air with a bent finger. "I knew all along. I saw what had happened in New England all those years ago, and I did nothing to stop it in my own backyard. I knew the bloodline and the way it spreads. Have you seen the children?"

"I don't understand the question."

"The children of these monsters are monsters. Twisted and grotesque. You're supposed to love all of God's creatures, but these... things... have nothing to do with God. The blood of unspeakable evil courses through the abominations. I should have acted many years ago, with blade and fire, and rid Keyport of the black underbelly."

"I don't know why we're here," Tina said. "I need to get home before my dad freaks out. He already dislikes Matthew. I can't imagine what he's going to say when he finds out I got out of his car and left him." Tina wiped a tear from her cheek. "I need to find Matthew and he needs to take me home."

"You can't leave," Father Rocco said. When Tina shrunk back like she was slapped, he tried to smile. "I'm not threatening you, child. I'm just being realistic. I don't think they're going to let anyone leave town tonight. Or any night."

"What can we do?"

Father Rocco pointed at the ruins of the church. "Somewhere inside is the tool we need to battle them. But I can't retrieve it."

"You keep talking so cryptically," Tina said.

Father Rocco laughed. "I'm sorry, child. I'm not trying to frighten you but I'm trying to stress the importance of every action. God has shown me the way to battle the Esoteric Order of Dagon in Keyport, and I can only do it with you." He looked at the blackened brick and wood. "If I enter the former church, which has now been taken over by something sinister, I fear I won't make it out alive. There is something lurking inside and it knows me. It doesn't know you, but I know you for what you are."

"What am I?"

"The child who's been sent tonight to turn the tide and keep Cthulhu asleep."

* * * * *

Four of the hellhounds were on the top landing of the ancient house when Harrison came inside, and they growled low at him but didn't attack. He hated them in the home but could nothing about it. Just like the rest of his life.

He dropped onto the dusty couch and put his feet up on the coffee table. He would fall asleep here another night and wake, sweating, from a dozen nightmares, each one more grotesque. Harrison had no intention of going up the steps to a bedroom and walking past the creepy framed picture on the wall. The priest had somehow fallen into it, and Harrison didn't know how and didn't want to know. He made sure he didn't look at the horror painted on the canvas.

As if in answer, there was a thud in the corner bedroom upstairs. Harrison was almost positive it was the thing that might be his grandfather… but he wasn't going to find out. Things were happening at such a frenzied pace and he had no control over anything. For the second time, his wife was being rowed out to the end of the bay to be sacrificed to Old Ones. Harrison didn't know what had gone wrong the first time and didn't care. The woman who appeared in the dark pit under the house wasn't his wife anymore. She was a shell of her former self, broken and lifeless, despite her breathing and muttering.

When the locals had come to his door tonight, Harrison had simply stepped aside and let them go into the basement. The priest and the biker, both unconscious, had been carried away. Harrison was sure they were both fish food now. His wife was put back into a rowboat as the men chanted and did weird things around her body. It was all confusing to Harrison and he did nothing about it. What could he do?

Nothing.

He tried to get comfortable on the couch, closing his eyes. He could hear the damn dogs above with their sharpened nails clicking on the wooden floorboards in the hall. They hadn't tried to bite him but they were making it known where he could and couldn't go in the house. It was quite unnerving. Harrison just wanted to sleep tonight and wake with the sun shining. It was always better in the morning. The nights were getting too long and too scary.

In the morning, it was like the night before had never happened, thoughts fuzzy around the edges. He knew it was happening but it was easier to waste the day on the porch in the sun and nap on and off, since sleep at night was so fleeting. The nightmares kept him from getting a good night's sleep, and the damn dogs, scratching around in the house and growling, unnerved him. Harrison was waiting for the time he woke from a dream with one of the hellhounds feasting on his fingers or something far worse.

Nichole was out on the bay and probably already being sacrificed or whatever they were planning for her. Harrison was amazed when she first came back, even as wasted as she was, but he couldn't help her. They were always watching him, and when he was even remotely nice to Nichole, the dogs would growl and someone from Keyport would knock on his door within the hour, smiling and talking pleasantries, and, all the while, make veiled threats to keep her safe but keep her in the pit.

Harrison was worried about the biker and the priest returning, too. He thought they both needed to be either killed or left in the hole, as shitty as that sounded. Even though he'd started out helping everyone, in the end his fear had forced him to turn on them. He became their keeper. And the enemy.

The priest wasn't so bad, because he was frail and had big ideas but no muscle behind them. Harrison was troubled by Bones, who was a pretty big guy and could do some damage. Harrison was in fear of his life. By yet someone else. This was all getting to be too much for him.

He went into the kitchen and decided he'd either look for alcohol and get drunk or find a weapon and end his life. It was that simple. He really didn't feel too emotional either way, because he was numb to it all now. A sharp knife would do the trick and get him out of this mess. Maybe the combination of alcohol and a steak knife would really be the answer.

"You suck," Harrison murmured as he entered the kitchen. One of the hellhounds was standing at attention between the pantry and the silverware drawer, and it began growling as soon as Harrison entered. "I got it. I guess I'll go lie down and get back to some nightmares."

* * * * *

"In here," he heard the little voice, and Matthew followed without thinking, slipping in the side door of the building. The strange wet noises following him from the dock were disconcerting.

He was plunged into darkness and nearly screamed when he felt something touch his hand. He was told to be quiet by the voice again. He felt a tug and was led through the dark, the wooden floorboards squeaking underneath him. He could feel the walls to either side of him, shoulders brushing against the wood.

A door was opened in front of him but he still couldn't see. Matthew tried to turn around in the pitch black and run the way he'd come because he was terrified, but as he spun he couldn't get his bearings on where he was and which way he was facing.

He felt his hand being tugged, more insistent this time, in the direction he was facing. As he stumbled along, he could feel drops of water hitting him on the head and face, which was unnerving. Matthew didn't know how long or how far he'd walked in the darkness when he saw a thin beam of light underneath what must be a doorway ahead, sloping down.

The door was opened a crack and a young face peered out, lamplight behind him or her. It was hard to tell in the flickering light, but Matthew now knew his guide was a small girl of perhaps six or seven, frail with long frizzy blonde hair, covering her face and running halfway down her back. She was dressed in a nightgown, dirty and gray.

"Come in but hurry. They're right behind you," the one in the doorway said.

Matthew started to turn and look back but his hand was tugged.

"Hurry, before it's too late. They are searching for you."

Matthew complied and entered the small room and took it all in as the door behind him was shut and three deadbolts pushed into place. He was in an ancient storeroom, with crates and sacks piled in all four corners. There was another door on the other side of the room.

Six small children were sitting on sacks or standing far away from the lamp set upon a beat up wooden table. They were all dressed in dirty clothing or sleepwear, and were all... off.

"What is wrong with you?" Matthew asked the one still holding his hand. In the light, he could see she was deformed: the left side of her face looked melted, the skin of her cheek stretched and hanging three inches down to her shoulder. On closer inspection, the skin itself was tinged a sickly yellow-green and he could see small scales jutting from her face.

The little girl smiled with perfectly white teeth. "Nothing wrong with me. You look kinda funny, though."

Matthew took a good look at all the children and the room and was horrified by the strange birth defects in each child. Two of the boys only had one eye, the other side of their face swollen, green-tinged and like clay. Scales between fingers and toes were predominant, and underneath at least one child's clothes were large humps or fins. Matthew couldn't be sure in this light and didn't want to see more than he had to. He wanted to wretch.

The smell of the room suddenly overwhelmed him. It reminded him of dead fish, very subtle but definitely there. An underlying rot he felt clawing into his nostrils. He moved to the far door, which he reached in two quick steps. It was also bolted from this side.

"What are you doing? Where are you going? Stay with us for awhile," one of the little girls said, her giant fishy eyes pleading with him. "You can't go that way. It leads to the bay, and Father is out there tonight and awake. He'll find you."

Matthew unlocked the bolts and opened the door, staring into the darkness on the other side. He could hear dripping water and the smell of the ocean was strong. He had to be under the streets of Keyport or maybe under the docks, and he knew the water of the bay was right in front of him in the dark. "Is this a dead end?" he asked.

"You could say that," one of the boys said as he struck Matthew in the back of his leg with a small sack, stunning him and dropping Matthew to one knee. "You're going to stay here with us until you're called. We need you alive, but not conscious. Do you understand me?"

All the children crowded around Matthew, moving in with rusty blades, rope and sacks as weapons. He was pitched forward onto his stomach and his arms and legs were pinned to the dirt floor.

"Why are you doing this? I thought you were saving me from whatever was coming for me," Mathew cried out before his head was pushed into the dirt.

He heard them laugh, some of them making sloppy wet sounds as they did.

"You jumped from the frying pan into the fire. The one coming for you was trying to save you... from us. We're finally able to be upstanding citizens and help Father in his time of need."

"Who are you?" Matthew choked out, unable to move.

The little girl, who'd initially led him down, bent and pushed his head so Matthew could see her. She was smiling. "We're the children of the sea. The kin of Cthulhu."

* * * * *

Tina gagged on the strong odor of charred wood, swirls of smoke still drifting from corners of the ruined church. She'd begged Father Rocco not to make her enter the church or, at least, to accompany her, but he said he couldn't. The look of fear on his face when he even leaned against the gates was scary to Tina. She prayed to God she had the strength to find whatever weapon, inside the church, they needed to combat this evil force.

She wished her father was here to guide her. While to outward appearances he was a dominating man, he was a good man who only had Tina's well-being in mind. Her father would never come out and say he didn't like Matthew, but Tina knew him well enough to know she was breaking his heart by dating someone like Matthew. Tina decided she would break up with him... if she ever saw him again. Everything going on right now was much bigger than her love life.

Tina asked God to help her as she moved through the rubble, no clear path to follow. She closed her eyes and sighed, willing herself to relax. God would show her the way.

Both side brick walls were still intact, although only about four feet remained. The back of the church had collapsed into itself, imploding and creating a pile of broken wood, brick and plaster twice as high as Tina.

"Be careful," she heard Father Rocco yell, but she was already around the makeshift pile and his words echoed around her. She wanted to laugh. Did he think she wasn't going to be safe?

"Don't worry about me," she yelled back, more to calm her nerves than anything else. She'd make a joke and watch her step. "I'm having a lot of fun in here. I'm just trying not to break my ankle."

Tina came to where she thought the altar had been and was surprised to see a gaping hole in the ground. It was as if a bomb had gone off, charred wood running the edges of the wound, with blackened cracked bricks scattered.

Just as she looked down into the pit, not expecting to see much even with overhead moonlight, she was startled to see a small flame flicker below. Before she had time to react, she saw a face in the soft glow of a lighter, a burly man with a red beard beginning to grow in, making him look crazy and/or evil.

The man looked up, holding the cigarette lighter over his head. "Hello up there. I don't suppose you have a rope handy?"

"Um... huh?" Tina finally asked, confused. She wasn't expecting anyone to be down there.

The flame flickered in the breeze. "I'm just far enough down here I can't climb out, and the walls are crumbling and pulling bricks down on my head. I don't know how I ended up here, but I could use some help. I'm guessing you aren't one of the crazy Keyport residents or you would have killed me or done something bizarre by now."

"No, I'm from Hazlet."

He laughed below. "I have no idea where that is, but, as long as you aren't a local, I'm happy. I don't suppose you have any strong men up there with you?"

"No, only a frail priest."

"Father Rocco?"

Tina smiled. "Yes. He won't step onto the lot, though."

"Tell him Bones said he needs to get some rope and pull his biker buddy out of this new pit. I traded one for another, it seems. I don't know how I got here. But I'd like to get out."

"Okay, I will let him know."

"I would appreciate it, ma'am."

Tina nodded, even though she knew he couldn't see her. "I suppose this is what God had in mind."

"What do you mean?"

"I was sent to find a weapon to combat the cultists, and I guess that weapon of God is you."

Bones laughed. "I guess so. Oh, and it is probably the three metal crosses, with sharpened ends, I have next to me. I'm guessing they'll do some damage to these Cthulhu freaks as well."

EVIL

"We're missing something important," Father Rocco Ignatio said to Bones and Tina. "The holy relic you brought with you."

Bones was carrying the sharpened gold cross and he shook it in his hand. "I think this will do just fine."

Father Rocco didn't think so. "The relic you brought to Keyport is what we need right now. I have no idea where it is, though."

Bones nodded. "I don't think we really need it, but in this town anything is possible. The person who probably had it last was Harrison, and he's gone off the deep end. I think we need to pay him a visit but I'm dreading it. From the beginning, he has creeped me out and I went against my senses and trusted him."

"The Lord works in mysterious ways," Tina said. She'd been quiet for the last hour, since the three joined together.

Father Rocco felt horrible for the innocent girl being swept into this madness, but knew she was a key to getting out alive and, hopefully, shutting down the evil that was Keyport forever. "We need to go back to the house and have a chat with Harrison. If he truly wants to save his wife, he'll be cooperative."

"I think Nicole is beyond help," Bones said, referring to Harrison's wife. The last time they saw her she was jabbering inside a pit under Harrison's grandfather's house. "And for all we know, she's been sacrificed yet again. This place gets weirder and weirder. I can't wait to be done with it and back on the road."

"I think, with the coming of dawn, we'll either be done with this or too far gone to care," Father Rocco said.

"Nothing like being positive, Rocco," Bones said. "It's only a few blocks back to the house, but the entire town seems to be mobile and will probably try to stop us at every step." Bones bent down and picked up a charred two by four. "I'm actually looking forward to busting a few heads, especially after they subdued me so easily the last time. I'm taking a few down before I go."

The three unlikely companions started heading east, staying in shadows and moving in fear.

* * * * *

When Harrison was summoned by Sylvia Smoltz, the realtor and wife of his grandfather's lawyer, he went without complaint. The Hell Hounds watched him go from the living room, growling when he didn't move quickly enough. He decided his last dying wish (and he hoped he'd be dead soon) was to take out as many of these stupid animals as he could.

They got into her car and she pulled out of his driveway.

"Where are we headed?" Harrison asked.

"Dylan wants you at the Broad Street Pub." Mrs. Smoltz glanced over at him with a clear look of disdain. "So far you haven't been much help to the cause, you know."

"I'm doing my best," Harrison said and laughed. He had no idea what he was doing and what they expected from him. "It would help if someone fucking told me what was going on, though."

"Don't use profanity," she said curtly. "I do not tolerate it."

"Oh, my bad." Harrison could feel his anger rising and his thoughts spinning out of control. "I wouldn't want to upset the crazy bitch taking me to the crazy guy who tried twice to sacrifice my wife to a water demon."

"Water demon?" She laughed. "Where did you get that nonsense from? The Great Cthulhu is our absolute ruler. You'll see." She glanced at Harrison again. "I just hope I can watch him rip you apart in person. You disgust me."

"I'm not so fond of you, sweetheart."

They pulled up to the curb outside the bar but Sylvia didn't turn off the car. "Go inside. Dylan is expecting you. Don't do anything stupid, Mister Marsh."

"Don't tell me what to do, bitch."

She gasped. "How dare you talk to me like that."

"Fuck off. The next time I see you, as God is my witness, I will punch you in the face," Harrison said and opened his door.

"Ha. There is no God, only Cthulhu. And you, sir, don't have the intestinal fortitude to put a finger on me. In fact, I dare say…"

Harrison punched the woman in the face, smiling when he heard the crack as her nose was broken. He was about done with this bullshit.

* * * * *

Matthew DiNardo sat motionless in the corner and watched as the children moved all around the small dirty room, fighting and playing and singing. He bled from dozens of small bite marks and wounds, but he'd live. He had no idea how he'd get out of this room alive, though.

He'd also managed to get most of his body behind a rotting pile of flour sacks, only his head showing. Inch by painful inch he tried to wedge himself deeper into the pile but the sacks were heavy, moist and teeming with cockroaches and tiny black spiders.

One of the little girls, her face melting into her neck, stopped and stared at him with a lopsided grin. "Do you want to play some more, mister?"

He wanted to wave her off with his hand but he didn't have the strength to lift it, and the last time he'd seen his mutilated fingers he'd wretched. "Not right now, honey. Why don't you run off and play? Or, better yet, is there an adult around I can talk to?"

She looked at him for what felt like ten minutes but was probably only one before smiling again. "I can ask my uncle if he wants to talk to you."

Matthew smiled through bloody lips. "I'd love to talk to your uncle."

"He'd love to talk to you, too," she said excitedly. "I'll send one of the smaller children to fetch him. Then we can all play. Uncle loves to play with our toys as much as we do."

Matthew didn't like the sound of what she was saying. "W-what do you mean?"

"Mommy doesn't like when he's down here playing with us sometimes. She says he plays too rough. I think he's fun."

Holy shit. "You know what? I think I'll be fine. I'll just rest for awhile and then we can get your uncle to play. Right now I just need a nap."

The little girl shrugged and went back to her friends, who were busy pulling apart a rat.

Matthew didn't know if burrowing in like an animal would work. He watched the children as they stretched the dead rat to obscene lengths, feet, tail and head popping off with sickening snaps and spurts of gore. When one of the boys took a bite of the torso Matthew puked again.

They'll drag me out with or without their uncle, and they'll rip my limbs off and eat me. Matthew thought getting to the door, no matter how painful, was the best course if he wanted to live.

Fear driving him and giving him strength, he pulled himself up onto his knees and ignored the pain.

"Hey, he's ready to play again," one of the girls said.

Matthew used the wall behind him for leverage, picking himself up. As the little girl moved closer, he kicked out and drove her across the room. As the children came at him, Matthew was like a possessed man, feet and hands in motion, clearing the area in front of him.

But there were too many, and one of them got inside his striking zone and bit him on the thigh. He fell to one knee and before he could pull the brat off him another leapt onto his back and drove dirty sharp teeth into his ear, tugging at it.

They were upon him now, sheer weight keeping him pinned.

"I want to eat his winky," one of them said. "I bet it tastes weird."

Matthew struggled but they were sitting on his arms and legs, keeping him down. He heard screaming and realized it was coming from his mouth. He was shouting as he tried to move.

"What's with all the noise down here?" he heard a deep male voice shout as the door opened.

"It won't shut up," one of the kids said. "We're trying to play with it, but it keeps making that horrible noise."

"Shut up or I'll make you," the man said.

Matthew went silent and stopped struggling. The kids didn't move.

The man was pale as a ghost, his skin rubbery and waterlogged. He had creases or gills on both sides of his neck, and he was naked except for a pair of dirty jeans. His stomach and shoulders were crisscrossed with ugly red slashes, and one eye was lower than the other. "If you make noise again, I'll tell them to slit your neck and be done with it. Where did you come from?"

Matthew was too stunned to speak.

"Are you alone?" the man asked Matthew.

"Yes."

"I mean alone in Keyport. Did you enter town by yourself?"

"Yes... no..."

"Which is it? I don't have all night. Is there a woman with you?"

"Yes," Matthew blurted. Why had he sold Tina out like that? To save his own skin. He felt like shit but if it was the only way for him to live... besides, she was long gone by now. She was safe at home in Hazlet, telling her minister father about what an asshole Matthew was.

"Where is she?"

"I'm not sure. I mean, let me go and I'll bring her back here." If they were stupid enough to let him go, he'd have a sporting chance of escape. All he had to do is convince this dolt he was better off alive than dead.

The man smiled, crooked teeth filling his mouth. "I don't need you to find her. Just knowing she's in Keyport is enough information. We'll find her."

The man turned to leave. Matthew didn't want to be left with these hideous children. "Wait, what about me?"

"Yes, what about it, uncle?" the little girl asked.

The man looked at Matthew with disdain. "Kill it before it makes another noise. Playtime is over."

* * * * *

Harrison was surprised to see Nicole, unconscious and lying on the floor behind the bar. "What happened?"

Dylan Murphy looked at Harrison's wife disgustedly. "She isn't worthy."

"Huh?" Harrison looked at the group of townspeople crowded into the Broad Street Pub. "Didn't you toss her into the water? Was my grandfather with her again?"

Dylan walked calmly to Harrison, standing at the edge of the bar, and put his hands on the man's shoulders. *His eyes are insane*, Harrison thought. *Or had they always been?*

"She's not what Cthulhu is looking for. We need to find another."

Harrison swallowed. He didn't want to die, sacrificed to some crazy monster in the bay. He decided he would need to fight his way out of the bar and run like hell until he was out of Keyport.

Dylan turned away and tapped the bar counter. He looked around at the assembled members of the community. "We need to find another female."

Harrison sighed in relief. He wasn't going to be killed by this cult of lunatics. But he needed to get away from them. A monster of a man was in the shadows near the back, hard for Harrison to see clearly. He'd just entered from a side door and began talking excitedly to a man, who ran to Dylan and whispered in his ear.

Dylan smiled. "There is another woman in Keyport who is not from here. We need to find her before its too late. Put out the word. I want everyone on the street tonight. No exceptions. We need to hunt this female down and get her to the boats. The Great One demands it."

Harrison had no idea who the woman was, and was hoping it wasn't the bitch he'd already chased into the pit. That one had gotten her head bitten off by the Hell Hounds. For some reason he wanted to snicker. He was losing his mind.

"Excuse me... can I bring her home now? Since whatshisname isn't interested in her as his bride or whatever the hell you cultists are doing."

Dylan stared at Harrison, making him quite uncomfortable. Just when Harrison was wondering how long the staring contest was going to go, Dylan turned and looked at Nicole. "Take her back to the house. There might someday be a use for her. Lucky for you, the blood of your superior relatives runs through your weakling veins. Or else you would have been taken care of as well."

"Ah, nothing like family to save you, right?" Harrison went to Nicole and lifted her off the table. "I'll see everyone later. You have a nice time torturing people and making asses of yourselves. Have at it! Viva Las Keyport."

Dylan pulled the holy relic from behind the bar and held it before him. "When we find the woman, we need to use this device on her."

"How?" someone asked.

Dylan shrugged. "Father will tell us."

* * * * *

Bones put his hand up to keep Father Rocco and Tina from moving from their hiding spot across from the Broad Street Pub. They'd been holed up about half an hour as people came and went inside, townsfolk carrying rifles and other assorted weapons.

When Harrison emerged, carrying his wife, Bones motioned for his companions to stay where they were. If they revealed their spot, they'd lose their advantage.

But now Bones was in a spot, because, if they followed Harrison, they could miss it if the bar patrons were on the move. But if Harrison had some information they could use…

He didn't want to split them up, either. The priest was no real use, physically, and the woman was too timid. If action was needed, Bones was the only one who could do anything.

Father Rocco came up next to him.

"Didn't I tell you to stay put?"

The priest smiled. "You said not to move as long as your hand was up."

"No, I said to stay where you were… oh, forget it."

"That was Harrison. Leaving with his wife, who we now know is alive. This is good news all around. Maybe he has some information. He was inside with the town people. We need to talk to him, right?"

"What if they let him go because he's working with them still? The last time I checked, he had us down in a hole with those killer dogs. He's not exactly someone I would consider an ally right now."

Father Rocco placed a reassuring hand on Bone's shoulder. "Have some faith, child. Did you see how mad he was when he left? And how he looked at his wife when he put her gently into the front seat of his car? He's no longer under their spell, I venture."

"We can't be sure."

"At this point we have nothing to lose."

Tina came walking up and squatted down next to the two men.

"Doesn't anyone listen anymore?" Bones asked. He closed his eyes. "We need to go back to the house and have a talk with Harrison, but we're going to do this my way."

"Would you kill the man if you had to?" Father Rocco asked.

Bones hesitated with his answer. He didn't want to lie to a priest but his answer would stir up some real trouble, and he didn't want to discuss the options on the short walk to the ancient house. "Yes. I will kill him if I have to."

"So be it." Father Rocco glanced up to the sky. "Lead us, Oh Lord."

* * * * *

Dylan Murphy watched as the congregation left his bar. He stayed behind and straightened the tables and chairs, killing time before the important work began. Soon enough, someone would find the woman and bring her to him. He didn't need to scour Keyport for her. It was inevitable someone would find her.

Tonight was the night to let Him rise from the bay and take his rightful place, and Dylan knew it meant the end of his life. He was ready for it. He welcomed it.

He went behind the bar and poured himself a double shot of whiskey, sucking it down with a grimace. Dylan didn't want to get drunk but he wanted to take the edge off. While he could smile through the thought of dying and act casual in front of the Keyport branch of the Esoteric Order of Dagon, he was… scared.

"Dylan, what do you need me to do?"

Dylan turned to see the hulking man framed in the doorway. "I need you to go below and stay there."

The man's eyes went into slits and his gills flipped angrily on his neck. "I can help."

"You can help by taking care of those below. You've done more than enough. I thank you, and He will thank you when this is all done. Tonight."

"I can send the children into the shadows. They can see what others cannot see."

"No," Dylan said curtly. He was sick of arguing with the man. "You will do as you are told. We all have to do our part in this night. You've done yours, and now it is time to listen to me." Dylan shook his fist. "Now, go below with the rest of them and don't come up the steps until someone calls you."

The man turned and disappeared. Dylan didn't like him, or the others like him. Freaks and mutants, they served a purpose but Dylan still couldn't understand their overall importance.

They weren't from the real families of Keyport. They were outcasts from the north, the weak and disgusting those in New England had no use for. Several generations later, they were all the more grotesque. Dylan didn't even know how many were living below, under the streets and in basements, crawl spaces and under the docks. Maybe as many as a hundred. And they bred like rats but usually died out before reaching their twentieth year.

He disliked having them underneath his bar and having to deal with them, although, maybe tonight he'd need their help if anyone outside of Keyport tried to stick their nose in what was happening.

Dylan smiled and poured another drink, watching the liquid swirl in his glass. He glanced at the phone at the end of the bar. He really wanted to call former friends and family in Rhode Island and let them know he'd won. The Great One was coming to see him and not them. He was going to summon their Master and they'd all die because Dylan Murphy had been chosen. After all these generations, he would be the one to set this into motion and enter a new age.

* * * * *

They came at the house from the west, fighting step by step through stunted trees and thorny bushes. Bones led the way, trying to clear a path for the priest and the woman. *This looked easier on paper*, he thought. They'd wasted too much time already, and if he'd known it was going to be so slow and his arms and face would get so ripped up, he would have strode down the driveway to the house and called out for Harrison.

"Stop," Bones whispered and put up his hand. He turned with a smile and looked at the priest. "I'm going to go and check it out. You do not move from this spot no matter what. Don't worry about my hand being up or down, don't worry about anything. Concentrate on standing in this spot and not moving. Can you handle that, Rocco?"

The priest smiled. "I think I can handle it." He stopped smiling. "But can you handle them?"

Bones turned to see at least twenty townspeople coming up the long driveway, brandishing weapons and flashlights. He could sense many more just out of sight up the road, and knew they were probably surrounded. "If we have to fight our way out, stick close to me."

Tina whimpered and ducked behind a tree.

Bones didn't move. He watched as the group went past them, some only fifteen feet from their hiding spot at the edge of the tree line, and walked up to the house. A few men in the group split from the main and went around either side of the house, surrounding it.

"What are they doing?" Father Rocco whispered in Bone's ear.

"I don't know, but I'm thinking they don't know we're here, so we need to stay out of the way. For now, we watch and try to learn something." This night was getting worse and worse.

Someone rapped on the front door of the house and within seconds Harrison was on the porch. The house was too far for Bones to hear what was being said, but from the animated arm-waving from Harrison it was obvious he wasn't happy. When one of the men tried to push past him, Harrison knocked him back off the steps and went back inside, slamming the front door.

"Now what?" Rocco asked.

"Nothing. We wait. Maybe they'll leave."

But Bones could see they weren't going to simply walk away and leave Harrison and the house. Two younger men ran back down the driveway and soon another group of townspeople were going to the house, spreading out on all sides.

"Open this door or we will force it open," the leader of the group shouted at the house. "Harrison Marsh, you will let us enter."

"Uh oh," Father Rocco said. "They aren't leaving, and they might end up hurting Harrison."

"I won't lose sleep over any of it," Bones said. "But, if we can get Harrison out alive, it will be better. But I don't think we're going to, if you ask me." Bones didn't know what their next move was. "I'm going to get closer to the house, but I swear to God, if you so much as move an inch or put her in danger I'm going to slap you, old man. Do you understand?"

Father Rocco smiled and nodded. "You want me to stay here, right?"

Bones gently lifted himself from the bushes, careful to not get anything caught on him and let it snap back. He stayed on the tree line to the west of the house, moving one slow step at a time. When Harrison opened the door again and Bones saw all eyes on him, he managed to run for thirty feet before dropping down near a severed tree stump, sliding behind it for coverage. He was only about fifty feet from the porch now, and, if he reached out, he might be able to touch one of the stragglers hanging near the back of the group. He knew if he was seen he'd be facing dozens of people hell bent on hurting him.

"What do you want? You're not coming inside. No way. This is my property and I own it," Harrison was shouting. "This damn town has destroyed my marriage, taken my hair and everything I had. It's destroying my family, and tonight it stops."

When the lead townsperson tried to grab Harrison, Bones could see the blade as it moved through the air. The man screamed as Harrison, using a long knife, sliced open the man's arm. The blood hadn't hit the porch floor by the time Harrison slammed the door yet again.

As they pulled the bleeding man off the porch, two men tried to shoulder their way through the front door. Bones could hear the wood splintering and knew it wouldn't be long before they gained entry.

He needed a diversion to get them away from the door, but didn't know what to do. He needed to think quickly, too. Bones decided to crawl around to the side or back of the house and see if he could sneak in a window. Maybe Harrison wasn't too far gone. He was obviously no longer working with Keyport.

Bones moved back to the tree line, squatting down and moving as slowly as he could. If he was spotted he'd be surrounded, and the mob was getting louder by the second. Between the attack and the closed door, they were riled up.

The front door shattered at the same time an old man turned and looked right at Bones.

"Hey, who in Hell is that guy?"

* * * * *

Father Rocco watched as Bones ran down the driveway, staying as far away from them as he could, while being chased by at least twenty people. Bones was fast but there were many of them, and they were spreading out as they moved.

Two women, holding golf clubs, ran by only a few feet from the bushes and Rocco had to duck. Tina made another noise but she wasn't loud enough for anyone to notice, especially with a few of the adults yelling for Bones to stop and others with crazy war cries. The crowd was in a frenzy and Father Rocco guessed the bloodlust would only grow in time.

"How many are left at the house?" Tina asked next to him, scaring Rocco. "We need to get inside before something worse happens."

"When did you suddenly wake up?" Father Rocco asked her but he smiled. He was relieved she was suddenly among the living. He didn't want to keep dragging her around with him, especially if he needed to spring into action. *Ha, when's the last time you sprung for anything?* He laughed at his own joke. "Are you ready to move?"

Tina nodded. She still had a vacant look in her eyes but Rocco could see she was cognizant of her surroundings for the first time in a long time. "If we stay here, eventually someone will spot us. If they get to Harrison and hurt or kill him, we've lost an ally. Not to mention his wife. She's seen things… maybe she can help us, too. And maybe they know where the holy relic is." Tina started crawling to the house, her dress getting dirty as she moved.

Father Rocco started to follow. Once again he was being led by someone but he didn't care. He was too old to fight or run, and, if anyone grabbed him hard enough, he was sure they'd break his brittle bones. It was all he could do to keep up with Tina.

They made their way to the back of the house. The back door was open and no one was around.

Tina stood and ran to the door. "We might be too late."

Before Father Rocco could reach the opening, Tina was already gone. He wanted to cry out for her but that would give away his position. Instead, he climbed the back steps one at a time, feeling his knees popping as he did.

He stepped into a disused foyer, rotting coats and old paint cans on hooks and shelves, the floor dusty save for a few footprints. Rocco followed; dread hammering him with every step.

When he got into the kitchen, he stopped to listen for noise but there wasn't any. It was eerily quiet, and he didn't like it. His mind was screaming to turn around and run out the back door and head for the hills, but he had to find Tina.

The kitchen led into a hallway which led into the living room and the front of the house. Father Rocco stopped when he saw the multitude of silent townsfolk jammed into the room, and a few of them turned to stare at him when he entered.

He looked up the stairs to see Tina, standing next to the covered monstrous painting, with a dozen townspeople blocking her exit up.

"Leave her alone," Father Rocco shouted. "Let her go."

"We can't do that. This is Cthulhu's will now. The girl will be the proper sacrifice. We've waited for so long." One of the men closest to Rocco was brandishing a long knife and now he waved it at the priest. "Go back to your ruined church, old man, and pray to your god who deserted you."

"Leave her alone," Father Rocco yelled and tried to charge through the crowd, pushing and fighting as he moved. But he was too old and fragile, and in no time someone had pulled him to the ground. The townsfolk began beating on his body, stomping him.

He could hear Tina crying out to him but then someone crushed the side of his head and everything went black.

* * * * *

Bones was out of breath, but he pushed himself to keep moving. He was getting ahead of the mob but they knew these streets better than he did, and he was sure some of them were flanking his sides. He needed to hide as soon as he could. He also knew he was running right back into the hornet's nest near the waterfront and Murphy's Pub.

He leaned against a building on Front Street, in view of the bar. He didn't know how many people were still inside and didn't know if it was wise to walk in there. He'd be trapped. But he could hear his pursuers and they were closing on him. Bones also knew they were going to surround him soon, too.

The little girl was in the shadows and smiling at him.

Bones gave her a small wave. He didn't want to move for fear she'd call out and give away his position.

She motioned with her hand to come to her. When he didn't move, she frowned.

"Do you want them to find you? They'll hurt you, mister."

Bones could see her aura and it wasn't pleasant. In fact, there was something really off with the child. But right now he needed to hide.

"What do you suggest?" he asked her.

She pushed at the shadows behind her and he could see a faint light through the now-open door. "Follow me. I'll make sure they don't get you."

Bones decided the little girl was the lesser of two evils right now... but not by much. He ran across the street and joined her. She flew down old wooden steps and he followed, keeping his eyes and ears open for trouble, which he knew was coming.

He could smell unwashed bodies and blood before he got to the bottom of the steps and slowed down. The little girl disappeared around a corner and now he could hear giggling children.

"Come on, mister, follow me," she yelled and laughed. He could hear snickering.

Bones walked down the rest of the steps as quietly as he could. He still had the charred piece of wood in his hand but it would be useless in close quarters if he had to fight.

When he came around the corner, he wasn't surprised to see the children but he was caught off guard by how many were there and their various birth defects. Most striking, however, was the veritable pulsating evil they were surrounded by.

Bones knew his mother would not be proud of what he was about to do.

As the first little boy, smiling with dagger-like teeth, ran up to him with arms held wide as if he wanted a simple hug, Bones turned the two-by-four in his hands and used it as a battering ram against the boy's head.

* * * * *

Harrison watched, from behind the men at the top of the stairs, in frustration. The old priest wasn't a bad man, and he deserved much better than being beaten to death by this rabble. This was all going very badly and he saw no way to do anything about it.

One of the men on the stairs turned toward him while the others went after the woman. Harrison supposed this was the female they were looking for, and she's walked right into their waiting arms. All was lost.

"You're coming with us," the man on the steps in front of him said.

"I don't think so." Harrison went to take a step back down the hallway to his wife but decided not to give up the prime spot at the top of the stairs. When the man came up another step, Harrison punched him in the face and smiled when he toppled backward, taking another man with him.

The woman was being dragged down the steps by two men but she was a fighter, kicking and punching and using her body as dead weight, trying to dig her heels into the banister.

Harrison charged them, tossing one man over the rail, where he fell a few feet and toppled a group below. "Run up the stairs and to the left," he yelled to her. "I'll hold them as long as I can."

She ran past him with a few people in pursuit, coming up the steps. "This is too easy," Harrison said loudly and began laughing. He didn't know if it was the frustration of being trapped in Keyport, losing his wife or the insanity he knew was taking him over, but he felt a great relief as he kicked the first man in the face as he came running up the stairs. "Bring it on, you sick bastards."

Harrison held onto the rail and steadied himself against the covered painting on the wall and used his feet to keep them at a distance. "I can kick the shit out of you cultists all day."

"Give up the woman and we'll let you live," one of them said.

"You don't get it, do you? I don't think I want to live anymore. Not after what I've seen. Not after the things I've done, and for what? To keep my cursed family name and help a bunch of lunatics raise a giant beast from the bay and destroy the world. Even saying that aloud makes me laugh. Doesn't it sound ridiculous to you idiots?"

"It is the way of the world. We need the girl in order to make it happen. Step aside."

"Nope." Harrison took a step up to get a better angle at kicking some teeth in and his hand slipped, pulling the covering off the painting on the wall. He instinctively looked away, closing his eyes.

He felt movement on the steps and opened his eyes to see two people, hands covering their sight from the painting, coming at him. It seemed like there were less people on the stairs, and the three previously in the lead were now gone.

The painting has claimed them, Harrison thought. He knew, if he was mad enough to look at the swirling mass of hideous colors, he would see the taken on the picture, writhing in horror.

"What are you doing?" someone from below yelled. "Don't do it!"

Harrison had yanked the painting from the wall and turned it to face the masses. He blinked and several people were simply gone. Everyone smart enough turned their gaze. Harrison kicked the closest person to him in the shoulder and toppled him and anyone underneath him.

As they fell, one of them men glanced at the painting and was gone. Harrison began taking slow steps up the stairs, angling the painting so no one would come back up the steps. "I will kill every last one of you if I have to and burn this city to the ground. Do you understand me?"

No one said a word and no one tried to go back up the stairs. He knew it wouldn't last long, but, if he could get inside the bedroom with Nicole and the woman, he'd be safe. For now. He needed to devise a new plan, and the painting was his best bet right now.

At the top of the landing, he stopped. "Do not think I'm bluffing. You are not my people and I'm ashamed to be called a Marsh. When I get out of this filthy place, I'm going to destroy every last remnant of the Marsh name and every last cultist I can find. Mark my words."

"You don't know what you are dealing with, Mister Marsh. You cannot win," someone yelled.

"We'll see." Harrison ran to the bedroom and opened the door. The room was barren and Nichole was in the fetal position under the window, rocking herself.

"Where is the woman?"

"Who?" his wife said distantly. "I'm all alone. All alone."

"Shit." He went back into the hallway and saw the bedroom door at the other end of the hallway wide open.

The doorway to the room his grandfather lived in… his dead grandfather.

* * * * *

Bones threw up. The smell of rotting fish and dirty bodies mixed with the blood was too much for him. He didn't want to see the broken bodies of the children and he felt horrible, but it was either them or him. They would have ripped him apart, as evidenced by the poor sap lying in the corner.

He didn't know how many there were and he wasn't going to count them. They'd come at him like a wave, the personification of evil in their inbred forms. He'd been around some bad people in his lifetime but his radar was off the charts in this place.

The board was cracked and splintered. Besides hitting these demon children, it had slammed against the thick walls a few times and he'd managed to knock one of the posts down. Bones needed to get out of this dank cellar before the ceiling came crashing down on him.

He got to the other side and started ascending steps slowly, but they were old and wet and making far too much noise. He knew if anyone above was listening they'd know he was coming up. All the noise from the battle below had definitely alarmed them as well.

And he heard someone moving above him now.

He finished breaking the wood in half. It would be easier to use it anyway. Bones stopped trying to be quiet and walked right up the stairs, putting his hand on the knob. He was amazed when he turned it and the door opened. He swung it and put his back to the wall, expecting an attack.

Instead, all he saw was an upper stockroom with two overhead lights and the biggest, craziest looking fucker he'd ever seen. And the monster was smiling at him.

* * * * *

"Holy shit," Harrison said and went back to the steps, suddenly appearing and holding out the painting. More people disappeared. "Go back down the steps or I will come down there and force you to look at this atrocity. Now, I mean it."

They backed slowly down the stairs. Once he was confident they weren't an immediate threat, Harrison went to the doorway at the other end of the hall, afraid to see what he'd find.

First Nichole and now this woman, he thought. *When will this end? How many innocent people will have to be destroyed before this madness is either stopped or their dark god is set free?*

Harrison would have to do what he should have done when he'd first gotten to the house: end his grandfather's unholy life.

The room was dark. Harrison reached in slowly and flicked the light switch, but it didn't work. He knew it wouldn't. The old man only came out at night.

"Grandfather? We need to talk," Harrison said. He slid the painting behind him, careful not to look at it. "I realize now what it means to be a Marsh, and I want to join in the fight and release our Master. I want us to succeed and thrive in this new world we'll be creating."

He didn't hear anything. He took a tentative step inside.

"Hello?" he finally said, taking another step, expecting an attack at any moment.

The blinds were drawn and he went to them in the dark, banging against a table or chair. He pulled the rotting blind, moonlight exposing the empty room.

"How is this possible?" He pushed over the table in frustration. The woman must have come in here. All the other rooms were locked.

He glanced out the window and saw the shadowy form of his bleached grandfather as he was exiting the house from the root cellar door, the woman unconscious in his arms.

"No," Harrison yelled. How had he gotten out and past him? Harrison stomped across the room to the exit and noticed the hole in the floor for the first time. His grandfather had slid down between the walls and, obviously, into the cellar. He was free.

By the time Harrison got down the stairs, the townsfolk had cleared out and he could see them as they made their way across his dead lawn to the bay and the rowboats.

* * * * *

The man (if you could still call it that) was a giant, menacing and with such a bad aura Bones almost couldn't see past it.

"Goddamn are you an ugly sucker," Bones said, more to keep his nerves calm than to really expect an answer or a retort.

"That's not what your mom said," the giant said through his cracked lips. He smiled again. "I'm going to enjoy ripping you apart, little man."

Bones was a big dude but compared to this guy he was small.

"Bring it. I don't suppose you'll take a bath before we begin, though? You stink."

"I'll bathe in your blood," the giant said and moved forward, hands moving and ready to pounce.

"Not very original," Bones said as he gripped the board with both hands. He'd aim for the eye and hope he could shove it into the thing's brain before sheer weight crushed him. "I'm going to ask you nicely to let me pass. I have no problem with you. I'm also in a hurry."

The man smiled and swept a hand to his side. "Since you asked me so nicely I'll let you go."

"Huh?" Bones took two steps to his side and away from the monster, still holding the board. "I just want to leave."

"It won't matter, you know."

"What do you mean?"

The deformed man pointed at the wall. "He's out there and He is going to awaken. Tonight. Right before us witnesses. You don't mean anything in the grand scheme of things, and neither do I. I could let you walk out the door and you wouldn't be able to stop it."

"Then let me pass," Bones said.

The giant smiled. "Ripping your arm off and beating you with it will just be a bonus for me on such a great night."

"Then it's going to suck for you that you'll miss all the fun," Bones said and moved suddenly, getting inside the man's range and jamming the ragged end of the board into his face, the piece splintering into his mouth and into the back of the throat. Blood and spit poured forth from the gurgling mouth of the monster, and Bones used the man's own weight against him, driving him back against the wall, where the monster closed his evil eyes forever.

* * * * *

Tina went with the old man willingly because God told her to. Despite his pale washed out skin and sunken red eyes, she was no longer scared. He was just an old man caught up in something bigger than the both of them.

When the townsfolk gathered behind them and followed through the dead grass and onto the small patch of beach, Tina began to pray quietly. She was calm. "I am the Lord's vessel," she whispered between prayers.

Dylan Murphy was standing with his hand on one of the rowboats, wearing a smile and holding the holy relic in his other hand. "Welcome. You should be very proud of what you are about to do."

Tina ignored him and went to step into the boat.

"Not yet, my dear," Dylan said and held up his hand. "There is a ritual tonight. We have a way of doing things. Events set into motion before any of us were born are now at their zenith." He looked out to the bay. "Tonight He comes."

Torches were passed around throughout the crowd, some stuck into the sand while others were held. Tina thought it was a bit dramatic to be doing this, even at night, but she kept her mouth shut. She was reminded of the old classic horror movies her parents had watched when she was a kid. She was never allowed to watch them, having to hide behind the house or under an end table while her dad complained about how violent and bad the movie was and her mom ignored him.

"We need to pray," Dylan said and held out his hands, motioning for Tina to take his in hers. She did.

The entire group joined hands in a circle on the beach, bowing their heads.

Tina didn't understand the words they began to chant but she shivered and knew their meaning on a primal level.

When she heard the words *Ph'nglui mglw'nafh Cthulhu R'lyeh wgah'nagl fhtagn*, Tina nearly fainted.

* * * * *

The Broad Street Pub was empty and so were the streets as Bones stepped outside. He knew blindly walking to Locust Street and the ancient house wasn't an option. An entire town filled with cultists was going to be between Bones and the priest and woman, and he didn't have the strength to fight everyone. There would be guards posted around the property.

If he took the time to crawl in, it would take over an hour and he might miss all the excitement. If he even got close enough. Before they went out into the bay...

Bones smiled and began walking to the dock at the end of the road.

* * * * *

Father Rocco wiped the blood from his face and winced when he touched his right eye. His body was one massive bruise, and at least three fingers on his left hand were broken and twisted. His sides hurt from all the kicks, and he guessed he had broken ribs. He heard himself wheezing and his left ear was ringing. He wouldn't be long for this world.

He dragged his body to the front door, crying with every inch. It was closed and he didn't have the strength to reach up and open it. Father Rocco tried to get to one knee but it buckled under him. He slammed headfirst against the door, adding a new pain.

"Jesus, help me in my time of need," he whispered. "Give me the strength to open this door and get to the bay before she is sacrificed to this evil entity. Give me the will to rise and open this door. Lift me up on high, Lord…"

Father Rocco, straining, could see the doorknob turning. *A miracle*, he thought, just before the door swung open and banged him in the head.

* * * * *

Harrison stared down at the priest and had to laugh. He'd heard him scratching at the door and thought a hellhound was trying to get out so he'd bashed it in the head. Only, he'd knocked out a beaten old man. The priest looked like shit. If it weren't for his frail chest rising and falling so fast, he'd be mistaken for dead. "I guess you are anyway," Harrison said. "We all are." He glanced back up the stairs where he knew his wife was still balled up and sobbing like a baby. She was gone to him now… she was dead like everyone else would be soon enough.

Harrison stepped over the unconscious priest and left the door open a crack. If the old man woke, maybe he'd crawl outside and find a nice quiet patch of dead grass to watch Cthulhu rise and die on. It didn't matter anymore.

"Honey?" he called up the stairs. Harrison was going to see his wife and spend their last remaining hours or days together. He didn't expect her to respond.

Nicole was still hunched in the corner and Harrison went to the window to open it but it was not only painted shut but nailed, too. He tried unsuccessfully to loosen it, finally pulling his sleeve down and smashing the glass out, letting the cool night air in.

When he was finished breaking the glass out and making sure nothing jagged remained, he bent down and pulled his wife up to her feet, leaning her against the wall.

There was a chair in one of the other rooms and Harrison carried it in and set it right in front of the now-open window.

"Come on, baby. Sit with me awhile and let's watch the end of the world together," Harrison said. "We'll have the best seat in the house."

* * * * *

Tina woke when they lifted her and put her into the bow of the rowboat. There were four men with her, all carrying torches and watching her intently.

Dylan Murphy was sitting beside her. "How are you feeling? We had quite a scare there for a few minutes," he said. "You banged your head."

Tina reached back and felt the lump on the back of her head, pulling her hand away and seeing the drying blood. "What have you done to me?"

"Nothing. You actually just fainted and hit your head on the boat. I'm glad you're alright." Dylan grinned, his face like a maniacal pumpkin in the torchlight. "We don't want you damaged for the sacrifice you will become soon enough."

Tina noticed the holy relic in Dylan's hand and knew she had to get her hands on it. Before it was too late. She looked back to see the lights of Keyport in the distance and knew she was far into the bay right now. They were the only rowboat out here and the water was calm. "What now?"

Dylan sat down in the rowboat. "We wait for Cthulhu to give us the first sign."

"Which is?"

"He begins to rise and we toss you into his waiting maw. It's pretty simple. Brilliant in its simplicity. We've already done the chants and the rituals and now it is up to him. You will give us what we need... what the others have failed to do whenever it is time."

"How many times?" Tina asked, genuinely interested. She was under the impression this was almost a given, that she'd be killed and then the monster would awaken. Now, she wasn't so sure.

"Over the years... whenever someone in the Order of Dagon thought He was ready, but I always knew they were wrong. It took me years to rise in the ranks and know where He really slumbered. Not to the north, but right here, secreted under the bay, and waiting for this dark night."

Tina closed her eyes. "My God - the one True God - won't let this happen, you know. He won't allow me to be a sacrifice to some dark power."

"You are about to be disappointed."

Tina opened her eyes just as Dylan began to chant softly and raise the holy relic over his head.

That was when the powerboat came out of the darkness and straight at them.

* * * * *

Father Rocco got as far as the porch and was able to pull himself up into one of the wooden chairs. Every inch of his body screamed in pain and he passed out once or twice from a jolt of pain. He was wheezing and he thought his lung was about to collapse, his throat gurgling with what he hoped wasn't blood. He was too old for internal injuries and knew there was no hospital run in his future. What little future he had left.

The townsfolk were mobbed on the shore, their torches and flashlights giving off weird glows. His old eyes couldn't see too far past them into the bay but he caught a glimpse of light out there and figured they were drowning the innocent girl and trying, once again, to summon their Master.

Father Rocco had nothing left to live for, but, despite this sobering fact, he was still trying to get every last breath he could find. He wanted to do whatever it is he could to help, even if it was only prayer at this point.

With slow, deliberate moves, he extracted his rosary beads from his pocket using broken fingers and wrapped them around the bloody digits. Father Rocco Ignatius bowed his head, tears streaming from his eyes, and in a hoarse raspy blood-filled voice began to pray for all their souls.

* * * * *

Bones killed the engine of the boat and let it drift right to the rowboat. He wasn't worried about stealth but apparently the four men with Tina were too focused on their unholy business or so arrogant they didn't think anyone would go against them.

He watched them watching him and they all looked unconcerned. Bones grabbed the rowboat with his hand, expecting them to attack him at any moment. No one moved but Tina smiled at him.

"What are you doing? It's too late. Join us. You have blood on your hands," Dylan Murphy said.

Bones gave him the finger and stepped onto the rowboat, being as careful as he could as it began to rock. One of the men reached out to grab Bones with the hand not holding his torch. Bones didn't know if he was trying not to fall or attacking, but he was taking no chances.

One elbow and the man pitched into the bay, his torch snuffed out as it hit the water. The boat rocked fiercely as the two other men tried to scramble away from Bones but Dylan just smiled.

"You're wasting your time. I can sense Him below," Dylan said and grabbed Tina by her arm, pulling her to him and threatening her with the holy relic. "Get back onto your own boat and go away. I'd run if I were you, because once she's killed and tossed into the bay, He'll rise and claim this world as his own."

"How about this," Bones said and took a step closer. The two men were between him and the girl. Bones cocked a fist and made to swing at one of the men, who jumped overboard. The other man followed suit, leaving Bones with Tina and Dylan. "I'll take the girl and then you join your buddies in the bay. We sail away and the sun comes up soon enough and we all live happily ever after."

"It doesn't work that way," Dylan said. "I kill her by drowning her. By this sacrifice, The Great Cthulhu awakens."

"What if I kill you first?"

Dylan smiled. "If you take another step closer, I'll drive this into her throat and choke her to death."

"You've never killed anyone, have you?"

Dylan's smile dropped.

Bones took a step forward. "Because if you had, you'd know it takes more than an idle threat to actually snuff the life from another human being. You may think you're stronger than her, but her will to live is much greater than you think. Also, her neck muscles are more powerful than your hands and she'll fight. She's not tied up and her nails are pretty long, so you'll need to watch your eyes. Women love going for the eyes, you know. If she's smart, she'll kick you in the balls."

Tina suddenly relaxed and kicked back as hard as she cold, connecting with Dylan's crotch. As Dylan released her and doubled over, Bones yelled for her to drop to her knees and grabbed Dylan by his hair, lifting his face and punching him in the nose.

As Dylan's nose exploded and blood coated Bones, the bar owner fell back and out of the boat.

"Help," Dylan screamed. "Don't let me die."

Bones reached out a hand. "Give me the relic."

"No."

"Then you'll drown."

Dylan, treading water, went under and drank water, coughing when he managed to come back up. "No," he repeated weakly.

Bones held onto the side and grabbed the relic as Dylan, busy trying to climb back into the boat, came closer.

"No! You have no idea what you're doing," Dylan said.

"What are you going to do with him?" Tina asked.

Bones stared at Dylan, the evil radiating off of him. "Nothing."

Dylan gave Bones a look of horror. "You're making a grave mistake," he said before sucking in more water.

Bones pushed away, using Dylan's head for leverage and forcing him underwater.

Without torches left in the rowboat, it was dark, only the moonlight helping Bones to see.

Dylan gurgled and sank.

"Is he dead?" Tina asked.

"I hope so. It won't stop the rest of these lunatics from trying to stop us once we get back into town."

"We could let the current take us away from Keyport. I could find a phone and call my dad. He'll come and save us." Tina sat down in the rowboat.

"We need to help the priest and Harrison. There might be more people being held in town," Bones said. "But getting away and getting help might be the smarter plan."

Bones heard a splash behind them. Tina looked as well, but it was only darkness in the bay and the waves slapping lazily against the boat.

It was followed by another splash, this one louder.

"Is it the barkeep?"

Bones shook his head. "I don't think so. Too loud… too big."

What looked like a tentacle rose twenty feet into the air, followed by two more. In the pale moonlight it looked slimy, wet and dark.

"What is it?" Tina shrieked.
"Not what... who," Bones whispered.
The water churned around them.

Rats In The Cellars

Armand Rosamilia

The agent, an old bent woman named Gladys, held the single house key to 26 Walling Terrace in her arthritic claw just out of my reach. She fixed me with the cold stare, some calling it the Stink Eye, or the *Malocchio*, remembered from my Italian side of the family. "Where did you say you were from?" she asked me again.

"New York City, my dear. I'm here for a month or two tops before I shuffle on to see the sights of Philadelphia."

Gladys shook her head. "One month." She held up a crooked digit. "Then I want you gone."

I smiled and bowed, not wishing to question her for this turn of anger toward me, especially as this seemed to be the only home currently available in all of Keyport. I imagine my slight British accent, which clashes with the fishing villagers' own New Jersey brogue, is off-putting to her. Clearly, while I was out and about the small bay town, many of the locals had stopped and openly stared at me. News of a foreigner travels quickly in holes such as this. Keyport seemed a return of last century, with no motorcars, no updated technology, and not even a short tow-line area for a small-class dirigible to be parked in an open field.

One younger man, standing outside the barber's shop but clearly in need of a shave, his trousers and boots stinking of gutted fish, asked if I knew who the President of The United States was. As if I was so daft to be inside his borders without knowing some basic history and information. Biting back my own acidic tongue, I answered simply "The Honorable Woodrow Wilson", and refrained from asking him who sat the throne of England, or even of my birthplace in Italy. I was sure he had no idea.

The kitchen area was the newest part of the house, adjacent to the foyer. I hung my overcoat on a single nail, resting my hat on the ledge above. The home consisted of two floors, and now I occupied the first. Past the kitchen and the ancient icebox was a smaller storage room. Chips in the unfinished wooden floor spoke of large dressers, trunks and bedposts that had been dragged repeatedly across it.

In the dining room were a hobbled oak table and four matching chairs in the direct center of the room. Otherwise, it was bare. I noticed again the crude markings across the cheap wooden floor, and spied several chunks missing in the corners. I gingerly tested the floor as I walked but it neither squeaked nor bowed under my weight.

The next two rooms were built side by side and obviously part of the original floor plans, with faded stripped wooden floors (hardly any of the markings) and lovely triple bay windows filling an entire wall in each room, from a height of four foot from the floor to a full sixteen feet near the ceiling. Both rooms were empty save a worn couch in the room which I stood and a thick mattress on the floor in the next.

A front door (which led to the wraparound front porch) was in the second room (the bedroom, thanks to the mattress) but I was told never to enter or exit by that portal. Instead, the side servant's entrance would suffice on the side street, which suited me fine.

After unloading my battered suitcase of clothing and personal effects, and placing my three new books I had yet to read (the latest from Colette, Shaw and Kipling) on the fireplace mantle, I decided to walk into town and see the sights.

It was still light, the September moon pushing through the fading sky before the sun finally dropped. A full moon, a blood moon, tonight. I wrapped my overcoat around me, glad I had decided to take it with me. Even several streets away from the docks but quickly approaching I could feel the breeze whipping through the town's alleys and back streets, the pungent scent of rotting fish cloying in the air. I feared, before heading to Philadelphia, I would need a change in clothing. No wash would get rid of this smell.

Kearny Street ended into Barnes, which sloped unevenly into Main Street, and due east from there I walked. At the next block I stopped at West Front and admired the hustle of the city, so close to the docks. Men rode by on the cobblestone streets with their mighty steeds pulling all manner of wagon with supplies: barrels of pickles, oysters and beer. The street was lined with businesses and apartments above, and there was more than one man or woman sitting on a windowsill admiring the chaos below.

A man stopped not two steps before me, ready to cross east, and procured his pocket watch.

"I say, is that a Piedmont?" I had to ask, knowing full well it was. My interest in watches and mechanical devices often got the best of me, and I hadn't seen a working Pie (as I liked to jokingly call them) since 1905 or thereabouts.

He gave me the same look that Gladys had given me before. His bland features softened under his derby. "A gift from my second wife." He held it out to me but wouldn't let me touch it.

"A gorgeous piece. If you turn it over, you'll see the initials carved into the underside near the base." I squinted in the failing light. "Ah, I wish I could see it better. These fine pieces are going up in value all the time, especially with his supposed death in Mexico recently."

"Death?"

Now I've piqued his interest. "Yes, of course. There's been civil war in Mexico, and Mister Piedmont had been there organizing the factory workers for his new line of time pieces. Sorry business, as it turned out."

"I had no idea."

"Yes, untidy days indeed." I made an exaggerated squint of the watch. "A shame." I pulled back. "You might be holding a veritable fortune there in your coat pocket."

He licked his lips. "Perhaps we could duck into a business and you could take a look for me?"

I put my finger to my lips and tapped as if in thought. "I was heading to find a strong draft, as it were."

"Then you'll want to hit the Mick's place," he said.

"That surely isn't the name of the establishment?"

He laughed. "He's our resident Irishman, owns the Murphy on Broad Street. He's a likeable enough fellow, been here many years." He eyed me suddenly. "There are many in town that sees you being here a bit queer, if you get my meaning."

I put on my best smile. "I assure you, my good sir, I am merely passing through on my way to southern ports and cities."

He thought for a moment before offering a handshake and a return smile. "Douglas Grandon, fifth generation Keyport resident. I own the tailor shop on Green Grove."

"Jeffry Ruggerio, at your service. I'm traveling down from New York."

He laughed at that. "That accent marks you as farther than that."

"Aye, good ear, Douglas. I'm of Italian decent on my paternal side. My mother was a Peabody of London."

"Of the famed Peabodys? Who built the dirigible classes of last century?"

I grinned, walking side by side with him down the street of Keyport. "Yes, although once the other companies took over, the name's cache had less attached to it, I'm afraid. My grandfather made too many bad investments, squelched much coin in a new airship that never got off the blueprint properly, and sunk money into a college in Massachusetts."

"Well, I hope you scrounged enough from your savings to buy me a pint of fine ale. We've arrived."

* * * * *

I felt like I'd stepped back in time: the dingy little bar was oddly-shaped, with alcoves and free-standing walls haphazardly tossed into the small room. Candles flickered on the tables, across the long, worn bar, and behind the bar in sconces, giving off choking smoke and little real light.

Grandon led me to the bar, where I sat on an uneven wooden stool and gingerly touched the darkened bar, countless spills and God knew what else etched on its surface.

The bartender, a barrel-chested blonde with a droopy moustache and thick arms, pointed at Grandon. "What'll it be, Douglas?" he yelled in a thick Irish accent, even though the room was quiet.

"Your finest." Grandon glanced at me. "And a mug of your finest for my new friend here, Mister Ruggerio. He's in from England by way of New York."

"Is that so?" the bartender said with a queer smile. He put two mugs before us and offered his hand to me. When I accepted, his grip was like a vice. "Dylan Murphy, owner of this watering hole. Planning on staying long?"

I nodded. "I've gotten a rental for a month."

"Only a month?" he asked, idly wiping the bar in front of me with a dirty rag.

I smiled sheepishly. "It was all the landlady would allow me. She was very, uh, adamant on that account."

A man nearby at a table snickered. I turned, shocked that two men, wrapped in their fishing trousers and stinking of a fresh haul of shrimp, had been there the entire time. I'd thought we were alone. Now I saw many faces, quiet, huddled over their drinks at various tables.

The man stood, made sure every eye in the room was upon him, and strode to the bar, and sat on the stool next to Grandon and away from me. He grinned at Murphy, who winked at him as he poured another ale. "Where ya stayin'?" he finally asked.

"Over on Walling Terrace."

More guffaws from the seated men.

"Wouldn't happen to be the one on the corner, now would it?"

I didn't like the way he was grinning, like he was waiting for the end of the joke to hit me with it, and the room erupt in laughter. "Yes. Number Twenty-six."

"My grandmother was there," he said and began laughing, joining the chorus of laughter.

"Enough," Grandon said and stood, waving his arms. "Leave our visitor to his cups."

"I don't understand," I blurted, knowing it would be better to drop this line of conversation but unable to.

"Most of our grandmothers and grandfathers and distant relatives of the past stayed there. Until recently, 26 Walling Terrace was the funeral parlor for Keyport," Grandon told me quietly.

The room dropped back into silence and I sipped at my drink, letting the heady foam curl around my top lip. I'd been around the world and back, and been in plenty of the ritziest establishments and the seediest holes, but never a place quite like this. It was odd, but since my brief time in Keyport I'd seen nothing but odd.

I decided to chat with my fellow bar patrons, forget what had transpired, and be the better man, as they say. I leaned forward and into Grandon, looking around him at my new friend at the bar. "How's the fishing out here?"

Someone behind me coughed, a low guttural noise like he was going to keel over any moment. The man at the bar put a weathered hand on his mug but didn't lift it, nor did he even glance at me. "By the by, you can't beat a fish pulled from the waters of Keyport bay."

"I cannot wait to taste the local delicacy. Is there a particular spot in town to find the freshest catch?"

He grinned and glanced at me, lifting his mug to his lips. "Aye. Head east a block and dive into the bay."

* * * * *

That night, feeling good after hefting a few pints with the locals, I strolled to my temporary home. I had no doubt I could win over at least a few of the locals given time, but did I want to spend my month here doing that? The city of Keyport was like a throwback to the previous century, with lamps on each main thoroughfare, but the town blanketed mostly in darkness. I could hear the clop-clop of horses a street or two over, and see many candles in the windows, even at this late hour.

On Kearny, just before the cross of Walling, a darkened house caught my eye. I couldn't rightly say why, but I stopped in the cobblestone street and stared at its dark windows and closed door. I shuddered, although I couldn't say why. A glance at the other homes on the block told me it looked just like any other. Yet…

I put my head down and walked briskly to my destination.

As I came to 26 Walling Terrace I began climbing the wooden steps when I heard the noise, as if something was scratching just below my feet. I'd neglected to light a candle before leaving, and the house itself had no exterior means of illumination.

The sound emanated from under or below the steps, but in this lack of light I couldn't see or remember if the steps were hollow or solid. I stomped a shoe onto the bottom step and it rang solid, as far as I could tell. The sound ceased.

Rats in the cellars were nothing new, especially so close to the ocean. I was sure a family of giant wharf rats was in the basement or crawlspaces. I hoped we could live for thirty days in mutual harmony.

The servant's entryway and kitchen were pitch black, like a dark cloth over my eyes. I struggled to remember the layout of the rooms, remembering too late where the kitchen table was as I slammed a knee against it. Cursing in the dark, I stumbled through the arch into the living room, rapping my hands on the walls, until I felt the mantle of the fireplace. I'd remembered a large tapered set of candles, more for decoration, in the middle of it. The Stryker, my ferrogasium cylinder given by mother in happier (and wealthier) times came in handy once again. I was sure if I searched I'd find some archaic flint set to light the candles.

I lit the candles and pulled once from its sconce, shining it around the room to ward off the shadows. I realized I'd been holding my breath since banging my knee, waiting for… something. Like a child, I went through the house and lit every candle and lantern I saw. I must've looked a fool to my neighbors, since the house was aglow in flickering flames and all the old shades not drawn.

Just before bed, feeling quite tired as I sat and read from Collette, my eyes burning with sleep, I heard the scratching again. It came from underfoot.

My initial thought was to retire for the night and ignore it, but when it grew more insistent I felt I had no choice. Taking my candle, I went into the dining room, where I could hear the bulk of the scratching now. There was one wooden door, which I'd ignored.

The door opened to a dark maw, with steps leading down into the abyss. A slight dust-laden breeze roiled before my eyes, as if in menace. My hand quickly pushed the door shut with a resounding bang and I took a startled step back, breathing hard. Never before in my life had I felt such evil, such a force as I felt below.

I knew now there were cellars underfoot, most likely the rooms where the dead had been interred and drained of their bodily fluids. I had no need to seek them out, especially on this side of midnight by light of a candle.

Placing a pillow over my ears, I wrapped myself tightly and just before dawn finally fell asleep. The scratching never ceased.

* * * * *

"Rats in the cellars? It seems possible." Dylan Murphy placed a shot of his finest whiskey before me on the bar.

I hadn't slept well, and when I rose the scratching suddenly ceased. I stayed for the next two hours, making a light breakfast of bread and butter, but all was silent.

I steered clear of the cellar door, dressing and taking a long stroll through town, ignoring the locals as they openly stared at me as I passed.

It was lunch time and I needed something solid to eat as well as a drink or three.

"They kept me awake all night," I murmured. "It sounds like a noisy lot of them. It must be an entire family down there, parading around."

"Did you see any when you went down the steps?"

I looked at Murphy like he was mad. "Did you think I'd go down the steps? Heavens no, my good man. Who would even think of something so preposterous?" I laughed at him.

My stomach growled as I drank the whiskey.

"Can I get you something to eat? It's not the best lunch you'll ever have but it's still better than anything outside the town limits."

I nodded and tapped on the lip of my shot glass as well. As he turned away I did the same, glancing around the empty bar. With the meager sunlight entering through the open door, it was much more pleasant than the night before.

There was a commotion just outside. When I turned to see if Murphy had heard, he was already gone to the kitchen. I stood and went out, shielding my eyes from the sunlight.

Only steps away, the bulkhead to the bay stood, gray and imposing, a full man's height. I went to it. It tailed away to my right and south, walling off the thin beach as far as I could see. To the left, the wall ran another thirty meters until there was a broken gap.

It was here that I noticed several of the men from the previous night, knee-deep in nets and fish guts, swarming over a trawler as it docked at the end of the pier. They were like ants, moving in straight lines from the boat to the small end-house to the side of the wall break, carrying supplies, ice chests and covered in blood.

The man from the bar - I'd never caught his name or stopped to ask - grinned when he saw me watching them, a small wooden barrel in his hands. "Come to make an honest day's work of your time?"

I waved at him, trying to return his smile, even though his shared no warmth. "Just enjoying the weather."

He handed the barrel to a man coming out of the end-house and strode to me. The stench of fish was unmistakable but I kept my wits about me, and ignored it. At this, I was no fool. The man was nearing hostility toward me, but I would not offend him.

"This weather?" he asked as he stopped and pointed east and the open water. "You won't be saying that by nightfall. There's a storm coming, a nor'easter. The shrimp and fish can sense it. They leap into the nets on days like this to escape the wrath of the sea, understand?"

I nodded, even though I had no idea what he was talking about. I was sure he was chiding me.

"Why are you here, in our quiet little fishing village?" he asked.

"Just passing through, I suppose."

"I suppose you work for the government. I suppose you're here for no good."

"Of course not. If I were a government employee I'd be here in style, no? I'm also a citizen of another country." I pursed my lips when he began to shake. I feared the man would hit me.

"We don't take kindly to nosy people, and those that watch us. I suggest thirty days sitting in that rat-infested house and then you be gone."

"Rat infested?"

He waved me off as he turned and went back to the pier.

"Ho, sir, what did that comment mean?"

He was already away, blending in with the others on the pier.

I turned back, hands shaking at his comment, when I saw the little girl's face just over the other side of the wall. To say it was startling would be an understatement. She was pale like the moon, thin, white and blonde curls flittering over her sunken eyes, and the only real color of her face were her thin red lips. The oddest thing, though, were the small appendages on either side of her neck, as if she'd grown gills, or had an extra flap of skin. When she locked eyes with me I saw only fear.

"Your food is ready. Come now," Murphy called from the end of the block.

I turned to him and nodded. When I turned back the little girl was gone.

* * * * *

Dylan Murphy was an airship pilot until 1895. "I didn't like it, the height. Isn't that amusing? A pilot afraid of being up so high."

I didn't speak of the little girl once I'd returned to the bar. A steaming bowl of seafood soup was waiting for me, along with another whiskey and a mug of ale.

"I heard Grandon mention you were a Peabody," he said.

"Still am," I said with a laugh. "On my mother's side."

"I knew your grandfather, believe or not. I was there, in Albany in '89, when the L7 went down. The man cried."

"I wasn't very close to him, I'm afraid."

"He was a great man." Murphy tapped thrice on the wooden bar. "I learned quite a bit from your grandfather, even in the end."

"The end? He's still alive as far as I know."

Murphy shook his head. "Perhaps his body, but his mind is not what it once was."

"Pardon?"

Murphy leaned across the bar and looked at me odd. "Once I found out who your grandfather is, I assumed he was the reason you were in Keyport."

"My grandfather lives in Massachusetts."

Murphy shook his head. "Not in two winters. He resides here, in Keyport. A block from the house you are staying."

* * * * *

Before I stopped I knew which house he was supposedly living in: the one that had frightened me the night before. Even in direct sunlight, with birds chirping in the oak behind the house and a lone butterfly before me, it was with a bad feeling I strode to the front door and timidly knocked.

I heard nothing stir inside. A distant buzzing caught my ear and I looked up to see, far away in the distant north, a dirigible. Stray wisps of engine noise floated to me in the still air. I wondered if it was an omen, me standing on the front steps seeking a grandfather I hadn't seen in years, after coming seemingly at random to this fishing village.

When the door suddenly pulled open with force, I nearly tripped and fell. Grabbing the doorframe, I stopped my embarrassing descent and labored to keep my knees from buckling.

"Can I help you?" the wizened old man filling the doorway asked. He was like a golem, with thick gray skin and a balding pate. His eyes were striking, blue like the sea, and menacing.

"I seek audience with Mister Peabody."

The monster shook his head.

I waited for a further reply but he simply stared at me.

"Can you kindly tell him a Jeffry Ruggerio, his grandson, is here to see him?"

Without a word he slammed the door in my face.

I felt my face, red from embarrassment and from the sun. The dirigible was a distant memory and the birds had stopped chirping. I felt suddenly alone, standing on the stoop, sweating.

Several minutes passed. I put my hand twice to the door to knock again but thought better of it. I hadn't seen my grandfather in far too long, and was never close to the old codger. My mother had always been cold to him, especially since her parents had gone their separate ways when she was young. While his money was always spoken of in high regard, I never heard a kind word said about the man himself.

The door opened so suddenly that my cap flew from my head with the wind's force it conjured. "He'll see you now."

The man moved back into the dark, leaving the door gaping. I retrieved my cap, folded it in my hands, and reluctantly entered. It would not be melodramatic to say that I feared for my life as I entered, for the oppressive air hung on me like a thick woolen blanket. It was dark, dust swirls in the air, and a sense of neglect permeating the very walls. I smelled mildew and rat droppings and... something ripe.

I was led into a gloomy living room. The windows were covered in thick brown rugs nailed to the wall itself. A small fire burned in the fireplace, the smoke curling at the feet of my grandfather, who sat in a chair.

The sight of him stunned me. Where, only a few short years ago, the man seemed alive, robust and filled with a burning sense of purpose, now before me was a shell. His hair, once full and golden, was gone save a few strands that fell to his shoulders. He'd lost half his body weight, it seemed, and his eyes, once vibrant, were black coals set in a skeletal head.

He didn't move and I feared the golem had brought me inside as a cruel trick, to show me the old man had passed.

"Come closer," I heard him whisper, his voice like crumpled paper.

I obeyed. A glance behind me told me the servant was gone. As there was no chair to sit and none offered, I stood before him and smiled. "Grandfather, so good to see you."

"Lies."

"Excuse me?" I muttered. He was always arrogant and always a bit of a character but he was never rude.

His left hand moved slowly to his face, fingers like gnarled bird claws. "Did anyone follow you?"

"I don't understand…"

He sat up stiffer in the chair and pointed a finger at the near window. "Is anyone outside even now, watching us?"

I had no idea what he meant. I went to the window and touched the makeshift curtains.

"Only peek out," he said in warning.

I did and gasped when I saw Douglas Grandon, the tailor, standing across the street and staring at the house. "I don't understand."

Grandfather coughed. As I turned to face him I heard the slightest scratching below my feet. I jumped, but there was nothing there but dust and dirt on the wooden floor.

He looked at me queerly with those beady eyes.

I pointed down at the floor. "I heard a scratching, as of rats."

His thin lips smiled, bloodless and awkward. "Those aren't rats, Jeffry."

"Then you do remember me? It wasn't so long ago that we'd last seen one another. Mother - your daughter - is still in merry England."

Grandfather waved a boney hand and grimaced. "No cares about that woman. Tell her she'll not get a penny of the family fortune, because it is gone. Gone, I tell you!" He began coughing again but as I went to him he pushed me away with strength I didn't think possible.

I left him until the fit passed. I went back to the window but now Grandon was gone, or hiding behind shrubbery or the far home. Odd.

"You will stay until after dark. It is no coincidence you are here, especially tonight. I knew someone would come." He frowned at me. "Better you than anyone, I suppose."

"I cannot stay until dark, Grandfather. I have many things to accomplish today."

"You stay."

As if on cue, the golem appeared behind me. I felt his presence before I actually saw him. He filled the only exit from the living area.

"I need to eat and fetch my books," I barked hastily, feeling trapped. I wanted to escape this madness, this evil old house and this crazy old man and his goon.

"Toland will fix you a meal, and I have a vast library in the next room. Sit down, read, eat, and have some wine. Tonight we will return to 26 Walling Terrace and all will be revealed."

I didn't bother to ask how he knew where I was staying.

* * * * *

After a large meal of blackened fish, hard bread and a mound of white corn, I had fought vainly to stay awake. At some point I fell out and I shuddered to think how I'd come to be on the dusty couch, covered in a ratty blanket.

We left Grandfather's home just before midnight. Toland, his servant, went ahead, leaving me to walk-carry the old man, who was as light as a feather, and his bones seemed as brittle as a robin's skeleton. I started to ask him a question but he shushed me like I was a child.

Fear and dread came over me as we approached my temporary home. I had a dozen questions rattling around in my head but was afraid to ask them aloud, for fear they would be answered truthfully and drive me mad.

What strange coincidence, what cosmic crafting, what disaster of Rogiere's Nutrinoamalgram supposed time machine had brought me to this queer fishing village, one I'd never heard of until a few days ago? Why had I found my Grandfather, who only hours ago, I was told was here and not where I'd assumed he was? It all made no sense.

My other, pressing questions would have to wait, as I helped my grandfather up the steps when we arrived at our destination. Immediately the scuffling below us began, and I could picture large chunks of rotting wood being ripped by vermin claws.

"They aren't rats," he said to me suddenly as if reading my thoughts.

"Then what are they?"

"The children. Carry me inside, where I will sit and tell you before I go."

"Go? What are you talking about?"

I led him into the dark kitchen and was able to find a suitable chair for his slight frame without hitting my knee or breaking anything. I lit a candle and placed it on the table just as Toland entered, unwelcome, into my foyer. Something gleamed in his hand.

Toland stood above and behind my grandfather and placed the stopwatch before him with a cruel smile.

It was Grandon's Piedmont!

"Did you read it?" my grandfather asked the servant.

Toland shook his head and smiled a cruel grimace of terror. "Alas, I cannot read. I was, however, able to get the tailor to pronounce the single word etched to its base."

"*Cthulhu*, I presume?" my grandfather asked with a smile of his own.

I had never heard this strange word before but it didn't stop me from shivering in fright. I was quite out of my comfort zone and element. The primal part of me screamed to fling wide the door to the house and run, run as fast and as far as my legs would take me, away from this madness and Keyport and the chaos it held.

"Give my grandson the papers," my grandfather intoned with his raspy voice. He fixed me with a hard stare, one I was sure in ages past had forced business associates and enemies alike to do his bidding.

As I took the bundle, wrapped in cheesecloth and further in large unmarked sheets of paper, I watched my grandfather for further instructions. This was all too much for me to bear, and I wanted to flee once again. The golem near the doorway surely sensed it, because he took a step back and watched me.

"After I am gone, you must leave immediately. They will come for us, the both of us, as well as Toland. The citizens of Keyport have tolerated me here long enough, and tonight they know what is afoot. They will begin lining the streets soon, and this former funeral hovel will be razed by morn. I suggest you not be in it. I have worn out my welcome."

He tried to stand of his own volition but failed. I took him by the boney arm and he gripped my shoulders suddenly and stood up to his once-full height and stared into my eyes. His black pits unnerved me but out of respect I refused to look away. "To the cellar and be quick."

I decided not to argue. This was all so out of my control and I was an unwitting co-conspirator in things I could not fathom. As I led him through the dining room Toland came from behind holding the candle.

"Once you are safely away, out of New Jersey, I wish you to read the words I've written and heed them. You are the last of the family that can break this curse, but you must be steadfast in your resolution."

Without preamble, Grandfather flung open the door. A hot draft roiled up from the dark abyss, and I gave up two steps in fear, thinking my skin would sizzle and slide off my face if I stood longer. He took the candle from Toland, smiled, and moved with surprising speed down the steps.

Before I could react Toland had pushed me aside and slammed the door closed, but not before I glimpsed the monstrosity.

It was amorphous, white like glowing ivory, and slick with vile wetness. And it oozed to my grandfather.

Before the scream died away Toland was dragging me back through the kitchen. "I need my things, my books," I stammered.

"You will leave with your life if you are lucky," Toland whispered in my ear. As we rushed out into the night I could see torch-bearers marching from two different directions.

He pushed me to the west and pointed. "Go through the bushes there, slip onto Main Street and keep heading west until you feel safe."

"Feel safe?"

He smiled. "Trust me. Once out of the town's hold you will finally breathe again."

"And what of you?"

"I am born here and I will die here. Keyport has always been my home. The ocean will claim my body before light."

* * * * *

In the weeks that passed fleeting newspaper mentions talked of two fires in the fishing village of Keyport, and even without the exact addresses I knew which houses had been torched. No mention was given about bodies being found, and no news of my grandfather was mentioned. For all intents and purposes he still resided in his home in Massachusetts. My mother never accepted any of my telegrams or letters, seeming to disappear suddenly.

It was all a strange business, but it made maddening sense once I perused my grandfather's rambling and sometimes incoherent diaries. I would have scoffed at his talk of family curses, Old Ones and the ties of Keyport to another city, Innsmouth, if I hadn't seen with my own eyes the horror at the base of those steps.

Indeed, many a fitful night was spent screaming and yammering about it, until I thought I'd gone mad. When I'd met Lucinda, it was as if the clouds had parted and she was my ray of golden sunshine. The dreams stopped and we lived in relative peace in Philadelphia, where I settled down and became, ironically, a horologist, working with her father in the family business and specializing in Piedmont repair.

I'd forgotten about the diary, the strange *Cthulhu* word, and Keyport itself, until my dear wife Lucinda, pregnant with our first, died in childbirth.

As the doctors talked to me of their regrets, and the child being malformed and pale as the moon, with strange protrusions emanating from her neck, and with her toes and fingers webbed and greenish, I knew. By God, I knew that I hadn't escaped the curse.

Now what?

Cthulhunicorn

Katelynn Rosamilia & Armand Rosamilia

Taffy the Unicorn was near Innsmouth and wanted to go swimming. It was a beautiful day and she saw a very inviting beach nearby.

Taffy decided to fly over and stay for a little while. When Taffy arrived, she looked around and saw that no one was there. She found the perfect spot to lay and nap for a bit.

When Taffy woke up she decided to go swimming in the clear turquoise ocean. The water was perfect and she was a terrific swimmer. She didn't want to get out but she was getting tired of swimming and she was getting pruney.

She got out of the water she wanted to build a sand castle but soon figured out that unicorns couldn't make sand castles because of there hooves.

Taffy saw several people that looked *fishy* coming down the beach, so she decided that it was time for her to leave. Taffy decided to get one more look of the ocean before she said goodbye. When she peered out into the distance, she saw an island. Before going home, Taffy decided to fly over to the island and see what it had to offer.

* * * * *

That is not dead which can eternal lie... but Cthulhu was sure growing bored after all this time. He spread out on the island of R'lyeh, which had risen from the ocean floor for the first time in aeons. Before nightfall, however, it would once again sink to the deepest bottom of the ocean and be lost once more.

Cthulhu wanted to enjoy some sunshine, maybe tan a few of his appendages and feel sand between his tentacles before it was all lost in infinite wetness. There was nothing worse than trying to play with sand a thousand feet deep.

He wanted to eternally lie... on the beach and watch the cute, puffy clouds pass overhead as the sun warmed his cold body and dried his moving parts.

As Cthulhu flapped his tentacles in the air and wished the clear blue sky was always this close (and, he realized, with some dismay, seeing the sky so close made him homesick... and home was so out of reach right now), he saw a bird up above in the distance.

The bird got closer, but it was too big. Maybe one of those monster creatures he'd seen hundreds of years ago? Giant teeth, huge wingspan like a flying killing animal.

Yet, as it came closer he saw it was a horse. A flying horse? It had a horn on its head, multi-colored wings and landed on the beach not far from him.

Instead of being scared, it said hello.

* * * * *

And so Taffy and Cthulhu fell in love. They spent the rest of the afternoon getting to know each other and having a good time.

Taffy was explaining her day at the beach when she mentioned how she couldn't make a sand castle. Cthulhu offered to make her one. She was excited to see how it would come out. When the castle was finished, Taffy was amazed. It was humongous and Taffy thought it was the most romantic thing she had ever seen.

As the sun set over the water, Taffy knew it was time to go home, and so did Cthulhu. Taffy and Cthulhu were so in love that they decided to get married on the beach that very same night.

Taffy was so excited that she was finally going to be married. She invited her whole family and all of her unicorn friends to the wedding.

The *fishy* people of Innsmouth rowed out to the island, the Esoteric Order of Dagon did the catering, Shub Niggaruth and Nyarlotep stood in as Maid of Honor and Best Man, and the Pickman Bakery of Massachusetts provided the wedding cake.

The wedding was so pretty and it was the one Taffy had always dreamed about growing up.

They spent their one and only night as a married couple on the beach together, watching the stars. Cthulhu pointed out which one he was from.

* * * * *

The baby had her fathers eyes. Oh, and his tentacles. Even though her hide was a weird color you couldn't really describe with words, she was still perfect to her mother. Most days and nights, while Taffy taught her daughter how to be a unicorn and also how to honor her father, they would sit on the beach near Innsmouth and wait for Cthulhu.

And pray for Father, roaming free…

The Terrible Old Man of Keyport

Chuck Buda

Jerry was itching for a drink. He glanced over at Richie who puffed away on a cigarette, with his foot resting on the passenger dashboard. Charlie napped in the back seat.

"I need a drink. Can we stop for something?" Jerry kept his eyes on the road as he spoke. He didn't want to lose control of the '55 Chevy wagon. It was cherry.

"I could use a snort. Let's find something in this Podunk town." Richie tossed the remains of his butt out the window and looked at the sleeping man in the back.

The men were good friends and had been since Kindergarten. They did everything together, including prison time. All three had decided long ago that they would take what they could without permission and without apologies. So there was the little mishap in Middlesex County. Six months later, they were back on the streets for time spent with good behavior. Now they were headed to the Jersey shore for some action.

The plan was to hit some places in Rumson and Avon on their way to Atlantic City. If they scored enough cash then they would try their luck on the casinos to double it. Technically, it was Charlie's plan. He was the brains of the operations. Richie always provided the muscle. Jerry was the lookout. Their system had worked well over the years with just the one hiccup.

Jerry cut off Route 35, opting for Amboy Road instead to avoid the typical shore traffic. Amboy Road eventually funneled into West Front Street in Keyport.

"This town stinks, man. Like the bottom of a tuna boat at low tide." Richie wrinkled his nose and rolled up the window.

Jerry laughed at the elaborate metaphor. His eyes caught a sign that indicated Broad Street Pub on the next block. He didn't bother to use the signal on the classic car and just turned down Broad. The pub sat on the corner. An ancient, brick façade belied an extensive existence, probably dating back to the last century. Jerry pulled into a parking spot between too very old vehicles.

"Wake him up." Richie pointed to Charlie in the back seat. Jerry rolled his eyes. Richie liked to pull rank and make Jerry do the dirty work. Jerry tossed an old bottle cap at Charlie. It bounced off his nose and the big paw shot up to jiggle the nose in a circular fashion. His eyes blinked open.

"Get up, sunshine." Jerry slammed the car door and the three men walked up the hill to the pub.

When they entered, it was as if they had been transformed back in time. The bar was dark and smelled of old cigars and spilled beer. An undercurrent of bay water permeated the doorway. The pub was small, barely enough room for a decaying pool table, a few scratched up tables with chairs and the grizzled bar.

Jerry wasted no time. He found a seat at the counter and immediately lit up a cigarette. Richie nuzzled into the stool on Jerry's right. Charlie remained at the door, like he was still in a fog from just waking up.

"Three of your finest. On this guy." Jerry ordered and thumbed at Richie. He seemed to enjoy the opportunity to give his pal a shot as retribution. Richie nodded at the barkeep. The man was bald with a long, gray goatee. He didn't look particularly pleasant. The kind of guy that the three friends liked to rumble with. But this guy's arms were pretty muscular. Jerry and Richie kept their mouths shut.

"You gonna block the fire exit or are ya gonna come join us?" Richie's tone betrayed aggravation. If there was one in their bunch who always took slack, it was Charlie. He nodded and sat next to Richie.

The men sat and smoked while they sipped their ales. An old transistor radio spewed polka music through a lone speaker. It looked like it hadn't been dusted in decades, bookended by two ceramic steins. Richie asked the barkeep if he could change the station, but the request went ignored.

"Man, am I glad to be free again." Jerry rubbed his calloused hands together as he smiled at Richie.

"Yeah, the air smells better outside the joint. Except in this town." Richie made sure to state the second part loud enough for the rest of the pub to hear. The bartender spat on the floor and continued cleaning mugs.

Charlie pulled a small pad from his pocket and scribbled some notes. Richie took an interest in the writing.

"What're you writing down there?"

"Notes." Charlie continued without looking up.

"I can see that." Richie's tone showed aggravation. "What kind of notes?"

"Some accounting. How much we can afford to gamble, eat and drink before we go broke in Atlantic City."

Richie shook his head. "And how much is that?"

Charlie scrunched up his face and slid the calculations across the bar for Richie to see. Richie's eyebrows shot up. "Then we'll have to hit a few more places before we enjoy the attractions."

"I gotta squirt." Jerry tapped Richie's shoulder as he slid his stool back. "Need anything from the men's room?" He joked with Richie.

"Yeah, let me know if you find anything down there." Richie shot Jerry a wise smirk which was returned with a grumble.

Charlie and Richie drank in silence. Every few seconds, the bartender shot the men the stink-eye. Charlie ignored it. Richie met the look with steely resistance.

A few minutes later, Jerry hurried over to the bar. He elbowed Richie and whispered in his ear.

"Hey, see those old coots at the table?" Richie casually glanced around Jerry's shoulder.

"What about 'em?"

"On my way to the can, I heard them chatting it up about some guy who is a bit bonkers."

"So?"

"So, when I came out of the can, they were talking about how loaded he was."

Richie faced Jerry. "Oh yeah? Loaded how?"

Jerry shrugged. "I don't know. They just mentioned this old guy named Pike who was losing his faculties. And they were wondering how he was going to divide up his estate amongst his relatives." Jerry tapped some ash and blew a plume of smoke at the dusty tin ceiling. Richie glanced at Charlie who hadn't heard any of the whispers.

"Change of plans, Charlie." Richie patted Charlie on the shoulder. Charlie just nodded and guzzled his ale down in one gulp. The barkeep came over to refill his mug.

"Say, Mac. You know where I can find somebody named Pike?" Richie realized his tone came off a little too familiar.

The barkeep put Charlie's refill down and leaned over the counter. Richie noticed the man's hands were the size of baseball mitts. His knuckles chewed up from brawling, or years spent lugging heavy cases of alcohol from the basement.

"Yup." The barkeep's eyes burned holes through Richie's face. The man's breath tickled Richie's mustache. Then the man turned and went down the other end of the bar.

Richie looked after him. He turned and shot an incredulous look at Jerry before addressing the barkeep again.

"Who wants to know?"

Richie and Jerry both jumped. A small, corpse of a man had managed to fit in between their stools without their awareness. The man's eyes were covered by the brim of his round hat. Tiny white whiskers dotted the man's chin and his breath reeked of rotten fish.

"We do." Richie replied, holding back some vomit from the overwhelming fish smell.

"Bring a pitcher." The old guy pointed over his shoulder as he made his way back to the small table.

Richie ordered a pitcher. The barkeep reluctantly set it in front of them with a disapproving leer. They pushed back their stools and all three men crowded into chairs around the old man's corner. Jerry filled the mugs and the two old men wasted no time draining their drinks. He couldn't be certain, but Jerry thought there were scales on the back of their hands. He dismissed it as the beer and the bad lighting playing tricks on his eyes.

"So?"

The old man smirked out of the corner of his mouth. "The name is Seymour Pike."

"Pleasure to meet you, Seymour." Jerry extended his hand.

"Not me, you imbecile. The man you were asking about." Jerry lowered his hand quickly, embarrassed. "Pike is one of the originals. Family goes back nearly two centuries in town." The old man's teeth made a clicking noise that unsettled the trio.

"Tell us about his wealth." Richie pressed on.

"What for? You aiming to steal something?" The old man's cohort finally spoke up. He, too, hid his face beneath the brim of a cabby hat. Richie sat up stiff, looking uncomfortable with the question.

"Just a weary traveler. Collecting interesting stories. Nothing underhanded." He grinned to satisfy the old men. Jerry topped off their mugs and the old guys drank them down as fast as they were filled.

"Pike is sitting on a wealth of old books. Originals, mostly. Tomes that could fetch much coin in today's collector's markets."

Jerry and Richie exchanged glances.

"The books are his real wealth. Of course, the house is full of exotic art works and rare treasures from the bottom of the sea." The old man leaned across the table and spoke in a hushed voice. "Nobody really knows how all the treasure made it from the floor of the sea to his possession." He nodded his head definitively to put an exclamation point on the statement.

"Sounds like a great tale. Mind pointing us in the direction of his home? I'd like to…interview him to learn more." Richie spoke softly to keep other patrons from overhearing his request.

"GET OUT!"

The shout froze the men in place. Richie watched the two old men snicker into their fists before turning to face the barkeep.

"What did you say?"

"Get out." The barkeep's voice was steady and lower than his initial bark.

Richie slid his chair back and sauntered to the bar. He made sure to let the barkeep see his anger in his eyes. Both men held each other's gaze for several long moments. "I don't believe that's the way to treat your guests."

The barkeep folded his large arms across his barrel chest. "You are not guests. You are strangers. And no longer welcome in my pub."

Jerry and Charlie formed a wall behind Richie. The three men faced the barkeep in menacing solidarity. They ignored the two old men who continued to giggle and whisper back at the table.

"What do we owe you? Wouldn't want to leave a bad taste in your mouth about out-of-towners." Richie dug in his pockets for cash.

"Nothing. Consider it your gift. Now keep moving through town. There's nothing here that should interest you." The barkeep pointed at the ramshackle wood door that blocked out all signs of daylight.

Jerry and Richie again exchanged glances and then smiled. They slowly made their way to the door, never taking their eyes off the barkeep. Charlie followed them out. He paused at the door before leaving. "This town stinks like dead fish." Then he let the door swing shut behind him.

* * * *** ***

The skies over Keyport had turned murky while they drank at Broad Street Pub. A grayness settled over the buildings and the air seemed to close in around the men. It felt like they were breathing under water.

The men quietly got into the '55 Chevy wagon. They rolled down the windows even though they all believed the town smelled bad. Charlie quietly sat in the back seat while Jerry and Richie lit up cigarettes in the front.

"How are we going to find this guy Seymour?" Jerry looked at Richie with smoke flowing out his nostrils.

Richie shook his match out and tossed it through the open window. He placed his right foot up on the passenger dashboard. "I can use a pork roll, egg and cheese sandwich. Let's hit a diner and see if we can scare up the address."

Charlie made a yummy noise from the back seat. "I love pork roll, egg and cheese." Jerry shook his head as he started the car and pulled out of the spot. Richie just chuckled under his breath.

* * * * *

They stumbled upon Keyport Diner after leaving the pub. The diner was practically empty. Two teenagers sat in a booth in the back corner. An old man, who stared a little too long at them sat at the counter, eating a slice of pie and chasing it down with a black coffee. Charlie led them to a table near the street. He plopped down into the booth and immediately went to work shuffling through the coin-operated music machine. Charlie loved to listen to the classics from Sinatra and Valli. He wasn't as fond of more recent Jersey artists like Springsteen or Bon Jovi.

Jerry rolled his eyes at Charlie. Richie picked up on it and chuckled. A few seconds later, a buxom waitress made her way to their table with a stack of menus.

"Can I help you boys? Maybe some coffee while you decide what you want?" She offered to hand them the menus.

Richie stared at her breasts for an inordinate amount of time. Then he spoke to her chest as she left them in his face. "Three orders of pork roll, egg and cheese sandwiches on hard rolls. Side of fries for each. And three colas."

The waitress seemed to enjoy the attention Richie paid to her. She winked at him and snapped her gum. "Comin' right up, sugar." She walked back to the counter, checking over her shoulder every few steps to make sure Richie was still watching.

"Mm-mm. Nothing like Jersey diners, huh fellas?"

Jerry rolled his eyes at Richie this time. "Keep it in your pants, Richie. We got business to attend to." Richie wiggled his eyebrows at Jerry.

"So how are we going to find out about this Pike dude?" Charlie piped in for once.

Richie kept grinning. "Oh, I think I can get the deets from that broad."

Richie stood up and made like he needed to ask where the restroom was. Jerry and Charlie watched as the waitress leaned forward, breasts spilling through her slightly unbuttoned uniform. She giggled at whatever Richie was telling her. Richie caressed her forearm while he leaned closer to her ear. If he was whispering sweet nothings then she was giving up sweet somethings. The waitress laughed out loud, an obnoxious, nasal laugh. Then Richie sauntered off to the restroom. He turned to wiggle his eyebrows at the guys again.

When Richie returned to the table, he let the suspense build for a while. Finally, Charlie spoke up. "So? Did you get the info on Pike?"

Before Richie could answer the waitress came back with three hot plates of pork roll, egg and cheese sandwiches. After she placed the dishes before the boys, she leaned down to whisper to Richie. "I get off at 10. You can come pick me up after you visit your Uncle Seymour." She brushed her hand across Richie's flat-top.

Charlie stared at Richie with his jaw wide open. Jerry shook his head at Richie while he took an enormous bite of his sandwich, wearing the ever-present grin.

"Unbelievable." Jerry threw a French fry at Richie in disgust.

* * * * *

The '55 Chevy wagon pulled up in front of the ancient home on Atlantic Street. The house stood apart from the surrounding single-story fishing bungalows. The Victorian-style mansion loomed against the starless sky. Each window appeared to be lit by a gothic lamp or electric candle, casting pallor shadows against the old glass. The men stared at the home, feeling as if hidden eyes watched over them from behind dusty curtains.

Charlie shivered in the back seat. "Creepy, man."

Jerry was suddenly glad he wasn't going inside. His job was to sit on lookout, with engine running for a speedy getaway. This would be one time when he wasn't jealous for having to wait in the car.

Richie wasted little time. He got out of the car and started to walk up the overgrown brick path to the porch. Richie didn't hear Charlie behind him so he stopped and turned to the car. "Charlie. Get your ass moving." Charlie hesitated a moment longer, his breath fogging the back window. Then he opened the door and followed Richie.

The front porch was mired in cobwebs and dust. It looked like it had been centuries since someone had crossed the threshold. Richie waved his hand through a web and cleared a path to the knocker. He lifted the iron and clapped it upon the door three times. The face on the knocker was some sort of octopus with tentacles swirling around its head. The eyes looked like they stared right through Richie's soul. He averted his eyes before he could change his mind about hitting this house.

After a minute or so, nobody answered the door. Richie reluctantly used the knocker a second time. No response yet again. Charlie leaned forward and twisted the knob. The door slowly creaked open. He looked at Richie and shrugged. Then followed Richie into the home.

"Hello? Seymour?" Richie looked around the foyer. Old paintings hung from dusty wires along the cloth wallpaper. He wrinkled his nose at the fishy smell that lurked amongst the décor. "What is with this town and the smells?"

Charlie ignored Richie's question as he picked up some relics that adorned the end table. The house was eerily silent.

"Let's get to work. The old coot must be at Bingo or something. Look for that treasure they talked about." Richie entered the parlor in the front of the house. It looked like a library. Floor to ceiling bookcases lined three of the walls. He noticed a few stuffed birds with black eyes which stared at him as he walked past. He found it odd that the birds were crows and vultures. Based on the sea port's history, he would have expected seagulls or herons.

Charlie opened a little jewelry box, set on the desk in the middle of the parlor. The ornate box was empty but for a few rusted fishing weights. He began opening the drawers on the desk, searching for anything they could pawn for quick cash.

Richie read the titles on the book shelf. The spines revealed many first edition classics like Twenty Thousand Leagues Under the Sea and The Rime of the Ancient Mariner. But his attention was drawn to a huge tome that leaned back upon a brass display stand. Richie thought that something urged him closer to it. He couldn't explain the feeling that filled his body as he drew near. He knew he had to touch the book. The one word on the cover perplexed Richie. Necronomicon. He had no idea what that meant. As he reached for the book, a voice startled him.

"Find anything...interesting?"

Richie spun around to find a frail man sitting in a red, high-backed chair near the window. He could have sworn that nobody else was in the house just a few seconds ago. Charlie audibly swallowed hard from the center of the room.

"Well? Have you?" The old man's skin was so pale that Richie swore it glowed.

"Uh, no. I mean, I guess so."

The old man stood up. His head hung slightly forward as his back hunched over. He didn't so much as walk as he glided across the oriental rug. "I'm Seymour, but I suppose you had already figured that out."

He was dressed in a black coat with tails. A frilled, white blouse rose up to his chin. Richie stared at the man's neck. It looked like Seymour had gills. Richie blinked and the marks were gone. The strangeness overwhelmed his sensibilities. He felt rooted to the floor.

"You aren't from around here, are you?" Seymour walked toward Charlie. He stared at the old man and replaced the small jewelry box on the desk. Charlie shook his head in response.

"Well, it would be rude of me to not offer you gentlemen a drink. Care for some Port?"

Charlie didn't speak. Richie answered for both of them. "We actually just wanted to hear some stories." Seymour faced Richie with an interested expression on his face.

"Stories? What kind of stories?"

"Stories about sea treasure. We heard some guys at the pub talking about some treasure you got from the sea."

Seymour chuckled. "You believe everything you hear muttered in a place full of liquor?" The question seemed rhetorical because Seymour continued without delay. "Yes, the sea contains many treasures. Some unnamed." He glided back to the high-backed chair and gently lowered his frame. "Please." He indicated that the guests should pull up a few chairs. "Rest your legs while I regale you a fine tale about the sea."

Mesmerized, Richie and Charlie sat before Seymour. Their plan to loot the old man now fogged over and nearly forgotten. They sat stoic, only blinking and breathing ever so slightly so that they wouldn't miss one syllable.

"This lovely town of ours has existed as far back as the colonies. Some say even longer. A few families chose to settle here. Fishing families. Folks of the water."

Seymour's black eyes darted between his two guests. He seemed pleased with their rapt attention. He rubbed his scaly hands together as he spoke.

"The Murphys were the first family to discover the ancient ones. They learned the language of the sea. And shared it with the rest of us." Seymour smiled. "I believe you met Dylan Murphy. Yes?"

Richie nodded slowly. He wanted to scream and run from the house. But he couldn't break away from the invisible tethers that bound him in place.

"Good. So Dylan introduced the Grandons and the Reynolds to the Old Ones. And also the Pikes. My family." Seymour paused to look at Charlie, who sat silently staring with haunted eyes. "I'll never forget the day I met Cthulhu. He was quite majestic. Inspiring, really."

Seymour Pike stood and began to pace behind his guests. He stopped behind Charlie and rested his bony fingers upon his shoulders. Charlie shuddered and tasted salt water in the back of his throat.

"You see, we are just mere servants in this world. We blindly go forward in search of love and fortune. It only occupies us until we are called. That…is when we truly come alive."

Seymour stalked back to the book case and retrieved the Necronomicon. He brought the ancient tome back to his chair and rested it upon his lap. Richie and Charlie were drawn to gaze at the over-sized book. It's textured binding beckoned their eyes.

Seymour opened the Necronomicon to a page with a hand-drawn image of a beast with long, gloomy tentacles. The writing alongside the picture was scrawled in quill ink. Words that could not be deciphered by the untrained eye.

"The sea is the bringer of life. The giver. We are born of its icy waters. We grow from the mollusks and the crustaceans to transform life into the land. And in the end, we return to the waters. We provide renewed nutrition to the Old Ones who call us back to our roots." Seymour lifted his hands in mock sermon. "The great god Cthulhu reassures us that in dying we live forever. In serving, we are served. And in darkness, all is brought to light."

Richie trembled. His skin crawled like thousands of bugs burrowed beneath his flesh. A clap of thunder rolled across the sky, shaking the gabled roof. The darkness outside the parlor windows painted the glass, obscuring the street lights. Richie managed to glance at Charlie. His friend's eyes protruded from their sockets. Foamy saliva bubbled at the corners of his mouth. His gnarled fingers dug into the wooden arms of the chair leaving white grooves.

Seymour Pike seemed to grow stronger with each utterance. The hunched countenance became more rigid. Even his pallor turned a rosy hue. The scales on the backs of his hands more prominent with silvery-green color.

Richie was horrified. He fought against the tidal currents. A watery death waited for him, somewhere toward the pier. Richie wondered how everything could have gone so wrong. Their little road trip to score money and women had turned into a death trap. Things unseen crept out of the corners to consume the living. A kaleidoscope of terror swirled around the men trapped in their chairs.

Richie thought of his mother. The poor woman would have to watch as they lowered his rotting corpse into the earth. That is, if they ever found his corpse. And he wasn't quite sure that would be possible. Thoughts of his mother crying over his grave provided just enough strength for Richie to fall to his knees. The inexplicable chanting paused as the old man appeared surprised. Richie worked his way to his feet to grab Charlie. His friend twitched and clawed the chair. It looked like it was too late for Charlie. Richie stumbled across the parlor, knocking relics from a coffee table. He looked over his shoulder at the old man. Richie thought that nictitating membranes clicked over the black eyes.

A rickety door opened from the back of the parlor. Richie strained to meet the eerie sound. His jaw trembled at the realization that one of the floor-to-ceiling bookcases served as a hidden passage to a dark portal. The waitress from the diner sauntered past Richie on her way to Charlie. As Richie watched her straddle his friend, two more figures brushed past him. The fetid smell of marsh water assaulted his sinuses. The two old men from the pub giggled as they closed in on Charlie and the waitress. Richie blinked furiously to clear the tears filling his eyes, only to witness the old men feed upon Charlie's flesh. The west sound of lip smacking and slurping sent chills down Richie's spine. The old men ate of Charlie's meat even though he was still alive, trapped inside the frozen spell of the Necronomicon's words.

The waitress cooed and glanced up at Richie. Her eyes blinked, a nictitating membrane sliding over her blackened irises before she leaned in to join the feast.

Richie screamed. The horror was too much to keep bottled inside his brain. He lunged for a shiny cutlass which hung across the parlor entrance. Swinging the heavy steel blade, Richie scrambled toward his tormentor. Seymour stood in defiance. The Necronomicon under his right arm while his left arm pointed at Richie. A bellicose wail reverberated around the parlor. Book cases rocked against the walls. Stuffed birds toppled to the floor.

Richie dropped the cutlass and fell to the floor. He clutched at his ears as the ancient horn wrapped itself around his brain stem. Hot fluids dripped between his fingers. He glanced at his hands and confirmed that blood was pouring from his ears. Richie's eyes glazed over, petrified in a colossal anguish. His head grew heavy and slumped to the old oriental rug. He smelled rotted fish in the dense fibers beneath his skull. Sea water drooled from his lips and puddled on the carpet.

Staring up at the cobwebbed ceiling, a new figure hovered over Richie with a sheepish grin. Dylan, the bartender, stood above Richie with a gaff in his hand. The large fishing hook was rusted with a scrimshaw handle etched with tentacles carved into its skin. Dylan grinned when he saw the fear blossom in Richie's eyes. He swung the hook down, tearing through Richie's mouth and tongue. Blood filled his maw and flooded Richie's throat, choking off his air supply.

Blackness enclosed Richie as he shrieked for salvation. The last thing Richie saw was Seymour Pike standing over him. Seymour laughed as he patted the bartender's shoulder with approval.

* * * *** ***

The screams startled Jerry so much that the lit cigarette fell from his lips and burned a hole in his lap. He fanned the burning embers to the floor and stomped them out with his heel. Jerry's eyes danced across the ancient home. The lamps and candles that had recently lit each window were no longer glowing. The windows looked like black, soulless eyes watching over him.

Jerry's chest beat hard. His breathing became erratic and he swung the car door open. He needed to find out what happened. He hoped the screams didn't come from his two friends. As he took a few steps toward the house, a clap of thunder rolled across the heavens. Jerry jumped from the sidewalk and landed against the fender of his car. Another shriek tore through the darkness, shaking Jerry where he stood.

He hustled around the hood of his car and dove into the driver's seat. His foot slammed on the gas pedal before he even shut the door. The tires screeched upon the asphalt, kicking up a strip which laid bare the old cobblestone beneath. Jerry never turned on his headlights. He was so scared, he forgot.

* * * * * *

The Broad Street Pub was busy. Keyport locals seemed to be in good spirits tonight. Like an unknown weight had been lifted from their shoulders. Irish music filled the background between mugs slammed on tables and roars of laughter. Dylan Murphy shined a few mugs and watched his patrons with pride.

Two men sitting at a table in the corner of the bar shouted over the din to be heard.

"Two of the bodies floated ashore. The eyes and tongues were missing, like they had been eaten away." The old man adjusted his round hat as he spoke. The other man, wearing a cabby cap, poured ale from a half-empty pitcher. "I heard the third body was found in the car that crashed into the pier. A sweet '55 Chevy wagon. The car was cherry." He slogged down his ale in one gulp.

"That body was just a husk of skin. No bones, no innards. They said it was like an empty burlap sack."

Both men repeated the gruesome details to each other like they forgot they had just spoken about it. The old men began giggling as they showed off the dark, bloody mustaches each wore upon their upper lips. The hairy souvenirs stuck only by the slimy flesh beneath the whiskers. As they ran through the highlights again, a hunched man at the end of the counter put two rare coins down upon the bar. He finished his glass of Port and placed his hat upon his head. The old man glanced at Dylan Murphy on his way out of the pub.

Dylan Murphy winked at the gentleman and slid the coins under the bar. He returned to shining mugs and enjoying the celebratory atmosphere in his establishment.

Lockbox

Armand Rosamilia

Three bodies, all torn apart like a pack of wild dogs had been through the apartment. I didn't think it likely, as they were on the second floor, above where the infamous A7 Club was located on the corner of East 7th Street and Avenue A. More than likely it was because of the wild pack of kids who roamed the East Village.

"Did you pull anyone from downstairs?" I asked a uniformed officer impatiently. I'd been woken from a nice dream and wasn't in the mood for wasting time. I knew what this was going to be: a drug deal gone wrong, or some of those hardcore kids from the bar looking for cash to buy drugs. It was all it ever was in this part of town, where the NYHC crew would terrorize and tag everything in their path like an ugly wave. I didn't get it, but my job was to solve murders and eventually get all of these damn punks off the street.

"We got twenty of them lined up around the corner in a vacant lot, Detective Graeme."

I wasn't looking forward to being this close to them. They were mostly street kids, and I considered them an unorganized gang. Most of them were skinheads and wore the uniform of choice: wife-beaters, Doc Marten boots and covered in seedy tattoos.

But it was better to talk to the street trash then hang out with the senseless violence inside this tiny apartment.

"Robbery gone bad?" Detective Briggs asked as he arrived late as usual. I knew he was a junkie and it was only a matter of time before heroin caught up with him and put his ass on these mean streets as well. Some guys never learned or kicked a bad habit.

"Doubtful," I said. There was cash on the dresser in the bedroom and the TV and microwave were still intact. The apartment hadn't been ransacked. Whoever did this wanted these three people dead. "Go talk to the landlord and bring a uniform with you."

Briggs scrunched his face, looking sickly with his sunken eyes and yellowed skin. He was visibly sweating despite the snow outside. "I don't need a babysitter."

"And I don't need a problem once you come down, right? Just do your job tonight without complications," I said. I didn't want Briggs anywhere near the street kids. All he'd try to do was score another connection in Tompkin's Square Park for later use. I thought 1983 was a bad time for drug use in NYC, but the first month of this year was even worse.

I passed a dozen NYPD officers on the steps as I went out into the cold night. This was the part of my job I hated the most: the lull between first look at the bodies and figuring out who did the dirty deed.

The kids were all leaning against the wall in a perfect line, which unnerved me. I was used to seeing them strung out on heroin, bouncing around, eyes darting back and forth.

"You search all of them?" I asked the nearest officer.

The cop nodded. "Every one of them is clean. No weapons. No drugs. Not even a pack of cigarettes."

"They knew we were coming."

"Nah. These cats say they're all Krishna or something weird."

"We're straight edge," one of the punks said.

I walked over and grabbed him by the arm. He didn't resist. I was going to make an example of the little runt but he didn't fight back, which pissed me off. "What's your name?"

"Ray." I noticed the punk had giant black X's written in marker on either hand.

I turned my back to the rest of the kids and the cops. This wasn't going to land us a suspect unless I played nice right now. The straight edge kids didn't curse, drink, do drugs, have premarital sex... nothing fun. "What happened upstairs?"

Ray looked over his shoulder to the rest of his crew.

"Don't worry about them. This is you and I talking. Off the record," I lied. "You know something?"

"Yeah. I know who might've done it. A guy named Ivor lived up there with his family. English guy with an accent like you," Ray said. "They'd only been in the country a few months."

I'd been in New York City since I was seven but the damage had already been done. My accent made me the eternal outsider, and as much as I tried to stifle the accent it was no use.

"Got a last name?" I asked out of habit. They'd find out who they were soon enough.

Ray shook his head.

"Where can I find Ivor?"

"He'd wander down to the club most nights it was open. Saw him at CBGB's last Saturday. He hangs out in the park until first light. He was a good guy. Never on drugs or wanting to fight. Just part of the crew," Ray said. "Can I go now?"

"Sure." I turned to the police officers standing near the punks. "They can go once you get all their ID info and write it up. I want it on my desk in an hour, too. We're burning time right now. We need to find out the last name of the son of the couple upstairs, too. Ivor something or other."

* * * * *

I found Ivor just after ten in the morning in Tompkin's Square Park.

His throat had been slit and he'd been dead for hours, propped up obscenely on a park bench facing the murder scene.

Even more players in this, I thought. It wasn't a simple suicide. He'd been attacked from behind based on the angle of the cut and the bruises around his shoulders and chest. Whoever had sliced Ivor open had made sure he was dead before letting go.

I shook my head when the EMT's arrived, hoping to save another soul. It was too late for any of that nonsense.

"We have a witness," Briggs said excitedly. The detective also looked sick. I was sure he hadn't pumped junk into his veins in hours and would be unbearable soon.

With such a big police presence, most of the transients had moved on to neighboring soup kitchens, abandoned buildings and other parts of town.

The witness was a teenage junkie female, who looked at Briggs on more than a few occasions during the brief interrogation. I was sure the two knew each other. *When this is over I'll head to Chief Russo and give him my concerns about Briggs again. Not that it will do any good*, I thought. Half the guys in the squad partook of the cheap street gear.

"What did you see?" I asked. I had no time for small talk. I wasn't worried about a killer rampaging the Lower East Side. I wanted to get home and be done with this long day already. And it wasn't even lunchtime.

"I saw that thing that did that to that guy," she mumbled.

She might've been a pretty girl before her teenage years and the needle had clashed. She couldn't look me in the eye and continued to glance at Briggs. I was smelling something fishy, like a convenient setup to name a perp Briggs had a hard-on for or something equally sleazy.

"What did he look like?"

"He looked really sick," she said.

"So does everyone else out here, honey. Including yourself." I glanced at Briggs, who was staring at the girl. Sick bastard. "I need to know what he did and where he went. Then you can go."

"He came up on that guy and took out a big knife and put his arms around that guy's neck and sliced his throat up. That guy just sat there while that other guy did that."

This was going nowhere. "Did the guy who did the slicing have any distinguishing marks? Tattoos? Wearing a skinhead uniform or have a shaved head? Was he black? White? Green?"

She visibly shuddered. "He looked very green. His skin was wet like he just came out of a pool. Bumps on the arms. That guy was a mess."

Leave it to drug addicts to make fun of anyone else, I thought. "Besides his green hue, anything else to make him stand out?"

"He took that guy's lockbox key from around his neck."

"You know it was a lockbox key?" I asked.

She nodded, staring at Briggs. "I used to have one myself." She touched her pale neck. "And had it on a thin chain around my neck, too. Everything I owned was in it. I had money and my birth certificate and baby bonds and my trust fund paperwork." She put her head down. "It's all gone."

Probably traded for a fix. "Thank you. You've been very helpful," I said. I turned to Briggs. "You have two hours to clean yourself up. Stay away from this underage girl and meet me back at the precinct in two hours."

* * * * *

I wasn't surprised when Briggs didn't arrive at the precinct. It was just another note I would take about the detective when I went before Chief Russo and tried to get his shield removed. The guy was worthless.

It didn't take long before the dead family had given up the ghost: they had a banking account three blocks from their apartment. I was sure their perp had gone straight there to retrieve the contents. He had a jump on me, but it didn't matter. Surveillance cameras or a bank employee who actually cared would help.

The banking building, located on Avenue A, was busy with customers in and out. I decided nice but firm would be the quickest way to get information. My British accent always helped as well, especially with the women. Not that I was a good-looking guy, but it made me infinitely more interesting once I smiled and began to speak.

The bank manager, a Miss Harriet, was like all the rest. When I'd flashed my shield she frowned. As soon as I began speaking, adding an extra layer of my homeland on for good measure, she invited me to her desk with a smile.

"We're looking for a man, perhaps who looks sickly, recently stopping into your fine establishment to procure the contents of a lockbox. All within the last few hours," I said.

"The privacy of our customers is of upmost importance to us, as I'm sure you understand," Miss Harriet said.

"And three gruesome murders not far from this spot would dictate I have not only the law behind me but common sense, as well as a Higher Power," I said, glancing at the ceiling. I'd noticed the bank manager's cross on the chain around her neck and matching small cross earrings. Religious folk always got scared when you brought Him into the equation, as if they'd be struck dead if they didn't do His bidding. It was quite convenient for an atheist like me. I put his hand in my inner jacket pocket, which was empty. "Should I share with you the pictures of the murder scene, dear? Several of my colleagues passed out when they entered the apartment, and not from the nauseous smell of death, either. It was the murders themselves and what was left of the bodies."

I almost felt bad doing this... almost. If I had to waste time going through the proper channels, inciting a judge to write a search warrant, jump through so many bureaucratic hoops like a trained seal, the killer would get away. It was better to cut a few corners for the end result than worry about all the proper steps getting there.

Miss Harriet was shaken enough to call in one of her lackeys, explain what I was looking for, and make pretend she had paperwork to do. She didn't make eye contact with me again until she handed me the man's address from the copy of his license.

I thanked her, making sure my smile was big and friendly. She didn't return it.

When I stepped outside and looked closer at the photocopy I stopped smiling.

Brendon Marsh. I had no idea who he was, but I did know he lived in Keyport. New Jersey. Quite a ride for me to take just to see if the guy had gone home.

I toyed with sending a couple of uniformed men down to do my dirty work, but decided I'd have to do it myself. There was something wrong with this entire scene and I wanted to solve this puzzle myself.

I got back into my sedan and started it up just as the police radio squawked.

"Detective Kirkpatrick? Graeme, old chap?" It was Briggs trying to be funny with a horribly mocking accent. I assumed he'd found a fix and was high as a kite right now. "Where are you?"

"I'm on my way to the Jersey shore," I said.

"Now, why would you do that? Already time for a little vacation?" Briggs asked.

I didn't want to keep chatting over the police band so everyone could hear us, and switching channels meant every busy-body on the force would switch with us.

"Meet me at the diner in thirty," I said.

"Which diner?" Briggs asked. He knew damn well what diner I meant.

* * * * *

We rode to Keyport in silence. Briggs stared out the window like a lost puppy while I tried not to lose it. I couldn't stand working with the guy, and for some reason the fact he always got involved in every one of my cases drove me mad.

I also knew we were wasting time. Brendon Marsh wasn't going to kill someone, steal whatever he was after, and calmly drive back home to relax. He was hiding somewhere, more than likely back in New York City. This was a wild goose chase, and to make matters worse I had to do it with Briggs.

When we pulled into Keyport it was like we'd gone back in time. I didn't see a fast food joint or a video store, one of those places where you could rent a VHS tape. Technology was beyond me. I still preferred a movie experience at the theater. Who wanted to watch a movie on your tiny television at home?

The few locals on the streets stopped and watched as we drove by, blatantly staring.

"Friendly town," Briggs said, finally coming down off wherever he'd been. I knew in another three or four hours he'd be ornery. Within six or seven hours he'd need another fix or I'd leave him wherever we were.

Broad Street to East Front Street and then left onto Beers Street and Walling Terrace was on my left, a maze of streets with older homes, perfect manicured lawns and more than a few white picket fences.

"This must be what they mean by living in the suburbs," Briggs said. "Very quaint. And creepy."

I found the address, and I have to admit I was both impressed by the size of it and also shaken by the dark cloud hanging over it. I couldn't quite put my finger on it. The house looked like every other one on the block and in town, with an aging porch and big bay windows. It had been painted in the last few years, and you might pass along on the road without noticing it.

But now that I was parked on the street next to it, I couldn't look away. It was as if the house was a mask, and something ominous was hidden inside.

Briggs opened his door and stepped out. "You coming?"

I shook off the dread and followed, each step closer to the porch and the front door like a lead weight tied to my shoes.

By the time I got to the door I was sweating and even Briggs noticed something was wrong, but he wisely kept his mouth shut.

I knocked, three quick strikes, the sound like a shotgun. I thought the wooden door would split, even though I hadn't knocked hard.

Briggs tired to peek into the windows overlooking the porch, but the blinds were all drawn.

I don't know if I expected Brendon Marsh to open the door with a smile and the contents of the mysterious lockbox in hand.

"Now what?" Briggs asked, taking off his jacket.

"We take the long ride home," I said loudly. I had no intention of leaving just yet, though. I don't know how I knew, but there was someone inside. Holding their breath, waiting for us to leave.

I motioned for Briggs to go to the car and wait for me. Surprisingly, he understood and went down the steps and strolled back to the car.

I put an ear to the door and listened.

Something tapped lightly, twice, inside. I banged on the door again. "I know you're in there. This is the police. Open up." I felt ridiculous saying such cliché lines, but they always seemed to work. I pounded on the wood again. "I'm not going to leave until you open up. We only want to talk to you, Mister Marsh."

I walked around the house, but the large windows were set too high for me to look in. They were all covered with blinds, anyway. I knocked on the back door but finally had to give up. If anyone had opened the front, Briggs would've seen it. If he were paying attention and not passed out in the vehicle.

Briggs was standing in front of the car with the hood up. When I approached he shook his head. "The battery is dead."

"How is that possible? What did you do?" I knew next to nothing about cars so when I stared at the engine all I saw was dirty parts connected chaotically. It took me a moment to see where the battery was.

I didn't believe Briggs. I got into the car and turned the key. Nothing happened. When I got back out I wanted to punch Briggs. "How did you know it wouldn't start? I told you to go sit in the car."

"It was getting warm and I wanted to crank the air conditioning. I don't have it in my car. I figured you'd be right back and we could drive home," Briggs said.

I looked up and down the street and back at the Marsh home. I was sure someone was watching us from behind the curtains. "Lock the car. We'll walk to the main road and find a payphone."

* * * * *

I was feeling generous and trying to keep calm, so I bought Briggs dinner. A seafood combination took me back twelve bucks apiece, but it was worth it. We stood near the docks, overlooking the bay, and ate while the fishing boats came and went. For a small town the docks were busy. This was a village that lived and died on their fishing.

As the sun started to fall over the horizon, I sighed. The car had been towed to the local garage but they couldn't get us a battery and wiring until the morning. An expensive call to the precinct with the last of my change had told me what I didn't want to hear: we were to stay in Keyport, do some digging and find Brendon Marsh. They didn't want the car left behind, didn't have the resources to send someone to pick us up, and Chief Russo had been vague about reimbursing us for a hotel room.

Since there were no leads in New York City and Brendon Marsh hadn't been spotted, the assumption was he'd used the lead time to come back to Keyport or he was in the wind.

My gut feeling was he was hiding in the house, but we needed to put some eyes on it. "I'm going to find us a room at the hotel a few blocks away. Lucky for us this is a small town and we can walk everywhere."

"What am I going to do?" Briggs asked. He was looking like garbage again and he'd have no chance of finding a fix in this town. I hoped for his sake he'd brought something with him, or it would be a long night.

"I need you to go over to the local police station and let them know who we are and what we're doing in town. Have them call Chief Russo, too. We'll need their help. We need to make sure Marsh doesn't slip away in the middle of the night. But finish your scallops first," I said.

After dinner we went our separate ways. I was hoping a visit to the local police would keep Briggs busy and out of trouble. I doubted he'd be able to score drugs in a town like this, but every drug addict I'd ever dealt with was pretty resourceful.

A quick walk around town told me a few things: I'd stepped out of the 1980's and into the early 1950's. This was a town caught in a moment of time, like a Norman Rockwell painting. Only, under the cute picture was something strange and maybe ugly. The townsfolk smiled at me but it was an act. I caught more than a few of them watching my moves from across the street. Even the few cars on the road slowed down, as if I had two heads.

I found myself back in front of the Marsh house.

The blinds on all the windows were still closed and the uneasy feeling came over me again, and I was already on edge from all eyes on me in Keyport.

I went up the walkway and steps and banged on the door, knowing it was a waste of time.

I also felt like this was a game and I was losing.

When I walked away I got two houses away before I stopped and turned suddenly, and I wasn't surprised to see the slightest flutter of a curtain in the front window.

* * * * *

Briggs didn't return that night. I sat on the bed alone in the motel, listening to the sounds of something in the walls and rain on the thin roof above me. The television looked like an antique and didn't get more than two fuzzy channels in. I turned it off within five minutes of trying to get the news.

I must've finally fallen asleep because a soft tap on the room door had me up and reaching for my service revolver before I'd opened my eyes fully.

I hoped it was Briggs, wandering in after a long night at the nearest bar, but I knew it wasn't going to be him.

There was a faint shadow under the door. I tried to slip off the bed as quietly as I could but it creaked and the shadow fled.

By the time I got to the door and threw it open the parking lot was empty save the steady drum of the rain. I stepped out and scanned the parking lot for movement. I could see into the motel office and the old woman who'd reluctantly checked me in was still sitting in the same spot staring into space. I was sure she wouldn't have seen anyone, even if she had. I was a foreigner with an accent flashing a New York police badge. Too many strikes in a small town like this, especially across the river.

A cop car hiding in the shadows at the far end of the parking lot caught my attention. I braved the weather and walked up, but the unit was empty.

"Hello?" I yelled. I was done with Keyport and Brendon Marsh and whatever the contents of the lockbox were. When no one answered except for more rain I retired to my room, but I wasn't alone.

There was a single sheet of paper, neatly folded, waiting for me as I opened my room door. It had been slipped under the wide expanse between the door and the floor and it was dry. In the few moments I'd had my back to the room someone had done it. I sat on the edge of the bed and read it.

Stop following me and leave Keyport.

Simple, direct and to the point. If it was supposed to deter me from finding Brendan Marsh it had the opposite effect. Now I wanted to capture the bastard and drag him back to NYC and charge him with murder and anything else.

I heard a car engine but by the time I rose and threw open the door I caught taillights of the police cruiser leaving the parking lot.

Great. Even the local police were in on this. They were circling the wagons around one of their own, and I knew the only way I was getting Marsh out of Keyport was to smuggle the perp out. Without a car and Briggs backing me up it was so much harder now. And they'd all be watching me, unless I acted quickly.

I went back inside and turned the dim light on next to the bed as well as the static television, then climbed out of the small bathroom window and circled the block. I ducked into bushes when a police car cruised by slowly, inching past the motel to make sure I was staying put.

It was slow going in the rain and I hid on more than one occasion when a local came into view. I didn't know who I could trust and didn't believe any of them was the right answer. It wasn't so much my cop instincts as it was my survival ones, and I remembered all too well growing up poor on the streets of Birmingham as a smallish child. The strong survived and the weak learned to run fast. I was still pretty fast even though I'd filled out over the years.

I walked past the garage the car was supposed to be at and wasn't surprised to see it not in the lot, and when I peered through the bay windows I saw it was absent. They weren't going to let me leave easily, and I had a chilling thought it was more than just me not being thwarted from catching Marsh. I wondered how far they'd go to stop me.

If I was smart I would've walked out of Keyport, hitched a ride to the nearest payphone or simply north and back home, but I'm stubborn in a bad way. If I walked into the chief's office without the car, Marsh or Briggs I'd get my ass handed to me.

Instead I was soaked by the time I arrived at the dark front steps of the Marsh residence. I took my time traversing the rickety steps, hoping the pounding rain would mask my movements.

The lights were out but I could see a flickering light in the front room.

Headlights appeared from down the block and I ducked, but the porch offered no real cover. If it was the nosy cop I'd be seen. I didn't think jumping off the steps would help because the lawn had no bushes or trees on this side.

The door suddenly opened and two bloodshot eyes peered at me, the figure stooped. "Come inside before they see you."

I didn't hesitate as the man moved and let me gain entrance. We both went to the blinds and peeked out just as the police cruiser went past.

"Thank you," I mumbled and turned to see him fully. "Brendon Marsh I presume."

He nodded. There was a candle light on a table. The room itself was sparse.

I blinked twice when I took his shadowy figure in because my eyes must be deceiving me.

Marsh had a sickly green tint to his skin, which looked wet. He was bent at the waist and looked to be in pain. I wondered if he'd been shot and had internal bleeding, barely able to stand.

"There is much to tell you and a short time. Once they realize you are here they will come. Then nothing will be able to stop them from entering this home," Marsh said.

"Are you ill?" I asked as he fell onto a well-worn couch but didn't offer me a seat. He looked like a bag of leaves, bumps and jarring bones riddling his body underneath his tattered clothes. If I didn't know any better I'd think the man had never been in NYC and taken such a long journey only a day or so ago.

"I've been spiked," Marsh whispered more to himself. He closed his eyes and with his heavy breathing I thought he'd fallen asleep until he began tapping his fingers on the couch. He looked much older than I knew he was, and his look was unsettling. I'd been on many cases with drug addicts and lost souls but Brendon Marsh was beyond all of it.

He turned his head and sighed, fear playing in his eyes. "They've arrived. We need to hurry. Let me up so we can go to the basement before it's too late."

I didn't bother asking why because he was reaching out a skeletal hand and I knew talking would only slow down whatever was about to happen.

I helped Brendon Marsh to the basement door and down into darkness as the first knock came to the front door.

* * * * *

I'm not sure what I was expecting: burning black candles, pentagrams in blood on the walls and floor, or a virginal sacrifice on a cold obsidian altar.

What I saw in the basement was much more horrifying... there was nothing out of the ordinary save for an ancient table with rusting tools scattered on its well-worn top and a file folder. A single weak bulb was suspended above the spot.

"This house used to be the funeral parlor for Keyport for the first hundred years," Marsh said and sighed loudly. "Many families died on this very table, the rest destroyed with the inbreeding." He turned to me and parted his dry lips as if to say more but stopped.

I looked away.

"What part of England did you say you were from?" Marsh asked.

I hesitated to answer the man for some reason. When he pressed me impatiently I told him. "Severnford, but I'm sure you never heard of it."

"Ahh, but I have. Directly northwest of Brichester."

"You've been there?" I asked.

He stooped suddenly and looked about to scream in agony.

I heard a crash above and supposed the front door had been breached. I needed to move this along and chatting about my origins made no sense.

He held up a finger. "I was there once. It's all it took. You know Brichester well, no?"

I shook my head. "I wasn't fond of the area. My family stayed clear of the odd things people said." I smiled. "It was a place we steered clear of. Even the unruly kids who wanted to find a spot to have a pint went south."

"The lake will corrupt," he said, almost as a whisper.

I shuddered. I'd heard this very thing somewhere a long time ago and I searched for the memory of it. "We're running out of time."

Brendon Marsh went to the folder on the table and opened it, showing the six handwritten pages contained within as he spread them on the table.

"This is what is so important? What you killed a man over?" I asked, incredulous. It wasn't bank or land titles. Deeds to anything. Simply mindless scribbles on old weathered sheets of paper.

"They needed to be destroyed before it's too late," Marsh said. "But I can't bring myself to doing it."

"Tell me what they are."

"Volume ten. Several pages ripped from one of the copies which can do great harm to those in possession," he said.

"I don't understand," I admitted. I could hear many feet running upstairs now. It would only be a few minutes before they found the upper level was unoccupied and found the door to the basement.

"Revelations of Gla'aki. You know. I can see it in your eyes. You were born too close to it." Brendon Marsh pushed the papers back into the folder and clutched the to his chest. "They need to be destroyed, but we need to escape first."

"We're trapped in the basement."

Marsh shook his head. "Through the small room to the west you'll find where they used to embalm and prepare the bodies for viewings. Underneath the slab you'll find a secret route to the original sewer system. It is no longer on the maps of Keyport but many residents know of its existence. We need to use it to run and find a safe area below so we can burn these wretched pages." He began walking to the west. "I have matches in my pocket. Why did I not burn them when I had the chance? Why do they torment me so?"

I followed to the room and slid the heavy slab to the side while Marsh watched, tears running down his sickly cheeks. "I'm cursed, you see. It is too late for me. Even now he calls me back to the lake to give back what has been stolen. They want the pages to complete their book before the Green Decay takes me."

I didn't know exactly what he was talking about but I could see the papers were of utmost importance to him and whatever he was babbling about.

"Graeme, are you down there?" It was Briggs calling from the top of the stairs. I guess he'd either gotten a fix or was about to fall. A part of me was unhappy to know he was still alive, to be honest. The man was a waste and if he was now working with the local Keyport police it could only mean trouble for me.

Brendon Marsh put a foot on the rusting ladder that led into darkness.

In one sudden move I grabbed the folder from his hand and pushed Marsh down into the hole and darkness. He didn't cry out but I could hear the thud below as his body found solid ground.

"Graeme, the police need to talk to you," Briggs was yelling. I could hear him coming down the steps.

I moved down the ladder into inky blackness and stepped on Marsh, or what I hoped was the man. I fumbled through his pockets in the dark and found his pack of matches. They would have to suffice for now.

The first one I lit showed me a wet tunnel and I had to stoop to traverse.

I clutched the folder as I began my escape, hoping they wouldn't find the tunnel above right away so I could make my way out of Keyport and find my way back to England and find out why these crudely written sheets of paper were worth killing for.

Dark Waters of Sin

Chuck Buda

Kenny's calloused fingers fumbled with the knot in his line. Dealing with tangled fishing tackle was difficult enough in the sunlight. It was even harder to fix in the darkness.

A stiff wind bit into his hands, numbing Kenny's fingertips. He dug his filthy fingernails into the nylon string. Ordinary fisherman would clip the line beyond the knot and start over. But Kenny couldn't afford to throw away perfectly good fishing equipment. Even a two-inch stretch of yellowed line.

He took a moment to collect himself before losing his temper. His eyes searched the heavens above for the familiar constellations which kept him company these last few years. Their brilliance was dulled by the glare of the full moon, which rode low along the horizon. It cast a whitish streak of luminance along the choppy waters of Matawan Creek.

The pause was helpful. Kenny smiled at the beauty of the moment, before returning to his task. It was important for him to stay focused so he could bring home some food, or money. Kenny had lost his job at the plant several years ago, and had struggled to make ends meet ever since. He lost almost everything since the day his employer dismissed him. First his wife, Gisele. Then the house. And then the car which he and his daughter had lived in for a few months. Although, Kenny hadn't really lost the car. Kenny had traded it for temporary accommodations and food. He finally swallowed his pride and applied for government assistance. Now, he and his daughter, Camille, lived in a roach-infested trailer. It was parked in a dumpy, fenced-in lot. The lot was situated in the backyard of someone's fishing bungalow. But the price was perfect for a man of simple means. A man like Kenny.

Kenny used the Keyport Fishing Pier in the wee hours of the night. He couldn't afford a fishing license. And the Fish & Wildlife Commission worked the piers and waterways religiously in order to protect the precious resources. Kenny didn't harbor ill will of the officers who did their jobs. He just figured out a way to work around the system. In Kenny's mind, he didn't catch enough fish to put a dent in the population. So it eased his conscience and helped him sleep during the day. Most times, Kenny caught very little to nothing.

His numb fingers worked the knot free and he sighed with relief. Kenny wondered what Camille would say if she watched him waste so much time untying a miniscule knot instead of cutting and retying. She would curse at him and call him a bum. Their typical communication pattern consisted of her complaining about his uselessness and how much he embarrassed her. The other children in the high school had cell phones and went on vacations. Camille had to create lies in order to hide the truth behind her lack of *things*. And she found it difficult to make friends with anyone for fear they would find out where she lived, and how bad the conditions were. Kenny felt ashamed for how he forced Camille to live. He had tried for so long to find another job. He had stretched all their savings and possessions as long as he could so they wouldn't have to move. But the sands of time finally filled the bottom of the hourglass.

Kenny hurled the line back into the creek. His eyes followed the bobber as it danced along the ripples. He prayed for some action tonight. It had been almost a week since his last catch. They were down to their last two cans of soup in the cabinet.

His life had become a trance-induced routine. Same thing, day in and day out. Kenny fished from midnight to five in the morning. If he was lucky, he peddled his measly catch to the fishmonger up the block. The businessman knew Kenny was not a professional fisherman so he paid Kenny at less than fair market rates. Kenny graciously accepted whatever he could get, so he could feed his daughter and pay the rent. If the catch was too small, Kenny would shuffle home and fry it up or pickle it to stretch the meals. The rest of the day was spent sleeping restlessly on the broken couch. Kenny allowed Camille to stay in the one bedroom. He figured it was the least he could do make her feel more normal. But once she came home from school each day, Camille would harangue Kenny whether he was awake or not.

The bobber jumped under the tiny wave and popped back up. Kenny's yawn broke while he slowly reeled the line in. It felt taut and his heart began to pound in his chest. He thought it could be a very nice fish on the line. As he worked the crank faster, Kenny felt the string fall slack. Whatever he had hooked had made a clean escape. Kenny groaned and finished reeling the line in to put more bait on the hook. He stared at the empty metal dangling from the end of his string. He glared at the dark waters and cursed his never-ending bad luck.

Kenny took off his knit cap and ran his dirty hands through his dark hair. It was quite salted these days as the grays became more prevalent. And his hair was getting much longer because he hadn't had a good haircut in months. Kenny told himself things would change soon. They had to. He couldn't be this unlucky for so long. The worm would have to turn for him.

Kenny chuckled to himself for thinking about worms. It reminded him to put another night crawler on the line and get back to work. He spread his arm wide and cast as far as he could.

The bobber danced along the choppy currents, glowing in the streak of cold moonlight.

* * * * *

"I can't believe my luck!"

Kenny flinched at the sound of his exclamation. His excitement caused him to shout louder than he had meant to. His terrible streak ended in glorious fashion. The ancient bucket was nearly filled to the brim with fish. And he had another one on the hook. Kenny squinted away his tears of joy as he reeled in the new catch.

Kenny had arrived at the pier, expecting a typical night of frustration. While he set up his gear, Kenny felt something in the air. Something seemed off. Even the creek smelled different. More acidic. Suddenly, a horrific sensation slid up his spine. Kenny's flesh chilled as his eyes searched the pier and marshy banks. A presence, lurking and watching him, pervaded the cool breeze.

He had dismissed the eerie sensations as ghosts of his bad luck. Kenny had prepared his line and he spoke to the dark waters beneath him. "Please let me have a good night tonight." He had stared at the choppy waves, imagining thousands of fish lining up to snag his hook. "I would sacrifice everything I have in order to bring home a bountiful catch." Kenny had closed his eyes and kissed the slimy night crawler on the end of his string. He swung the rod wide and cast a beautiful line.

The bobber disappeared into the darkness. Last night's full moon was absent, hidden behind an overcast sky. The heavens were black with no spark of starlight visible. Kenny focused his vision along the choppy waters to find the red and white bobber.

While Kenny dangled his legs from the pier and watched for a nibble, something insidious grew near. An ancient god had come home in search of new beginnings. It hid beneath the icy cold whitecaps, watching. The softly spoken wishes of the man on the dock brought it promise. The ancient one was interested in fulfilling Kenny's desires. For a price.

A slippery limb broke the surface of the water and slithered up the wood, feeling for Kenny. It clutched his leg and wrapped itself around him, wetness soaking through his pants. Kenny started to scream when an enormous being rose from the dark waters, towering over him. Cold spray misted upon Kenny and the pier. Kenny's scream caught in his throat as he tried to figure out what rose before him. He thought it had to be a dream. Maybe he had fallen asleep while fishing. Until he noticed the eyes.

Glowing red orbs glared at Kenny. Smooth, green slime surrounded the piercing eyes. Dark appendages twisted and reached for Kenny. He couldn't make sense of the towering figure with its slithering octopus arms and thinly veiled wings. But he could feel the power within the beast. It absorbed all light and thought. Kenny understood what the creature was. It represented everything as it had been, and everything as it would ever be.

The ancient one groaned and slid below the rocky waves it had created. Kenny was dragged along against his will. The great creature took Kenny beneath the surface. As the icy water filled his lungs, it showed him what was possible. And it made Kenny understand the truth behind promises. Even promises made to the wind. It showed Kenny that true gods were always present and listening. Especially when they were unseen.

* * * * *

Camille paced the cramped trailer. She was worried about her father. He hadn't returned from the pier yet today. On her way to school in the morning, she noticed he had never come home last night. It gave her hope that he had caught some fish. After school, Camille realized her father still hadn't returned home. She had checked down by the water to see if he had continued fishing into the afternoon. She thought it unlikely since he didn't own a fishing license. But she made herself check for peace of mind, at the least.

The flimsy door to the trailer creaked. Camille spun to see who opened it. Her father stood in the doorway with a wide grin on his face. His eyes appeared to have sunk into the back of skull.

"Where the hell have you been? I've been looking all over for you and I'm sick to my stomach with fear that something happened to you." Camille stomped her foot with her hands on her hips. She noticed a vacant look in her father's eyes. A shiver worked its way up her legs.

"I had a very good night." The words came out slowly and deliberately. Camille thought his voice sounded like an echo within a long tunnel.

"Great! At least YOU had a good time while everyone else was worried. I hope you managed to catch something so we could ALL enjoy some fun staying in this crappy trailer." She waved her hand around to sarcastically indicate their massive wealth. Camille's eyes watered as she tucked a curl of black hair behind her ear. The tears were mostly relief for her father's safety.

Camille's father raised a dirty fist in front of his face. In his hand was a stack of cash as thick as a deck of cards. Possibly thicker, Camille thought. She dropped her jaw and ran to her father. Her hands grabbed at the wad of money. Camille fanned the bills in front of her eyes, counting several hundred dollars. Her words caught in her throat.

"It was amazing." Her father licked his lips. "They kept biting. I thought I had lost my mind. Then I figured I must've had magical worms." He shuffled to the crooked couch and plopped down into the seat. Dust particles lifted around him.

"But…how?" Camille dropped the money on the table and kneeled between her father's knees. He caressed her cheeks as she implored him to tell her more with her hopeful brown eyes.

He burped. Camille wrinkled her nose at the sulfuric odor which passed his lips. He apologized to her, searching the ceiling for the words to his tale. Camille thought his breath smelled like rotten seaweed.

"It was darker than dark last night. And I had a weird feeling…"

Camille cut her father off. "Wait. Why are you just getting home now? Did you go drinking with some of the money?" She grimaced with distrust. Her father took to the bottle when her mother walked out on them. But he had been sober ever since.

Her father laughed. "No. Be still while I tell you what happened." He scratched the back of his hand and Camille thought his skin looked puckered, like he had been in the bath too long. "I felt like I was being watched even though I was all alone on the pier. But I fished anyway. We need money. And food."

Camille nodded and rolled her eyes. She hoped he would get around to the good part of the story. And soon.

"I wished upon a star for good luck but there were no stars at all. The sky was dark with clouds. And then the fish, they kept coming and coming. I never had a chance to take a break."

Camille clapped her hands. "So you found a new spot where all the fish are?"

Her father shook his head. "Nope. Same spot I've been fishing all along." He smiled at Camille.

"Is this a joke? What really happened?"

"I told you like it is."

Camille wanted to believe her father, but it still seemed too incredible a tale. Her disbelief must have registered on her expression. Her father's expression sagged.

"Come with me. I want to show you where it happened."

"Dad, I have to take a quiz in the morning. And it's late. I need to get some studying in now that I know you are safe. I couldn't concentrate all day."

"You must come. It won't be long. It's too amazing to keep it to myself." Her father's eyes twinkled like a little boy revealing a secret adventure to one of his friends.

Camille argued against going down to the docks at such a late hour. But her father insisted and so she relented. She knew she could badger him if it took too long, and she would force him to bring her home to study.

He placed the stack of money from the table into his pocket. His excitement left the trailer with him as began to walk without waiting for Camille. She grabbed her sweatshirt off the back of the chair, slipping on a little trail of water upon the floor. Camille glanced down at the streak of wetness and wondered where it had come from. The water dotted the floor from the couch to the door. She figured the water must have leaked from her father's boots. It seemed like a lot of water for someone who only sat on the pier. Camille shrugged and closed the door behind her without locking up. They had nothing worth stealing in the trailer.

* * * * *

An icy gust of wind bit into Kenny's face. It made his eyes water a little. He glanced at Camille as she tugged her sweatshirt tighter to keep herself warm. Kenny patted the plank of wood, indicating his daughter should take a seat on the pier. She hesitated for a moment and then lowered herself to the dock.

Kenny took a deep breath. The chilled air gurgled in his lungs as it mixed with the sea water. He felt a surge of excitement wriggle through his muscles. The time had come to share his adventure with his beloved daughter.

Kenny re-enacted the previous evening for Camille. He ignored her huffing and eye-rolling at his dramatic interpretation of the fortuitous event. A squish of water overflowed his soggy boot. He began to repeat the words he had whispered to the night.

"Dad, I get it. Now, can we please get home so I can study?"

Kenny continued to speak to the wind. He ignored his daughter's pleas. The ancient one would soon be here. And he couldn't wait to show Camille. As he continued repeating the words, the dark water in the creek began to swirl and splash along the banks. The wind gusted and then stopped almost instantaneously. The frigid night air became still and thick. Whitecaps along the surface grew larger, and the pier began to tremble as if a powerful engine chugged beneath the dock.

Camille jumped to her feet and ran for her father. The mark of terror was upon her face as she reached for him. But she never got close to his body.

An enormous wall of water shot into the sky, bringing the ancient one with it. Its towering, slimy visage looked like a wet effigy of some horrible scarecrow from the sea. Camille fell to the planks and screamed in horror. The suction of the creature rising from the depths of the ocean washed out the sound of her voice.

Twirling appendages, like suctioned octopus arms, rose before the scaly head which filled up the sky. Camille remained statuesque under the glowing red eyes which penetrated her soul. Tentacled arms plucked her off the pier, lifting her high above the place where she last stood.

Kenny murmured the words again and again. His eyes focused on the dark waters, oblivious of his daughter's plight above.

The ancient one bellowed and sunk beneath the disturbed surface of the creek with Camille in its grasp. Water plunged around the gap where the mighty creature had just been. The whitecaps rose violently at first, before settling. The waves carried away the turbulence across the distance. An icy wind returned, tossing Kenny's unkempt hair. His words trailed away into the night. The night became still once more.

Kenny shook with fright. His new master would always have that effect on him. And while he feared the ancient one, he respected its power and wisdom. He knew if he did the ancient one's bidding, then he would be taken care of. His days of empty buckets would be finished. Forever.

He thought about his daughter and how much he would miss her. Kenny's eyes watered. He knew Camille would come back to him someday. But she would never be the same. Kenny figured it would be okay. Camille would understand. In the long run, this would be best for both of them. No more worries. No more silly jobs or schoolwork.

They would both have one purpose. A true calling, which would prove to be more fulfilling than anything they had worked so hard for in this world. Camille would finally have a home. A place she belonged. Someplace she could really be proud of.

And time would be endless. For both of them.

Author's Notes

Keyport, New Jersey is a real town in central NJ, right on the coast. It is a small fishing town, with some great seafood from the Keyport Fishery, and some really old spooky houses.

I lived there for about two years in my twenties in a former funeral home that was definitely haunted. The town is like a postcard from the past, one of those places with some real personality. I grew up in the area (I'm a Belford boy) and we'd go to Keyport quite often.

And it was the perfect place to set a Lovecraftian series of short stories without having to make up too much. Trust me, I didn't have to stretch the truth too much...

I also want to thank my daughter, Katelynn Rosamilia, who was an invaluable assistant in the actual typing of "Ancient". I paced the living room while she typed my words, put up with my failure to tell her when a period was due and kept mixing up 'question mark' with 'quotation mark' when dictating. She is the best speech recognition software I've ever had, and she understands my Jersey accent.

During the story she even added a few suggestions and told me when a line didn't make sense. She's eleven and loves unicorns, so when she suggested the unicorn line and I added it she was happy.

During a much-needed break in writing (while swimming in the pool) we started talking about how funny a mash-up story with our favorite things (her unicorns and me loving Cthulhu) would be and "Cthulhunicorn" was born. We finished writing it in about an hour, Katelynn in charge of writing the unicorn parts. She saw how tough it is to write a story from scratch, then. Not too easy, is it?

The bonus story, "Rats In The Cellars", is one of my first attempts at a steampunk tale. When I wrote it (originally submitted to an anthology) I hadn't yet started the *Keyport Cthulhu* series, but you can see some of the ideas were already in place in my head. I decided to keep the story as-is, instead of changing it to better fit into the series. I think it is a great story that stands on its own, and I hope you agree.

And I want to thank Mr. Lovecraft, who scared the crap out of me as a teenager, and kept Cthulhu and the creatures locked in the crypts, inside the walls and under the dark deep sea in my head after all these years. I wanted to bring the Cthulhu stories out with my own twist, making them modern in a place that I knew well, and a place that a reader could walk down Broad Street in Keyport one day and say… 'Yeah, this place is cool, and creepy, and ancient.'

And so ends the Keyport Cthulhu saga… or does it?

It was my intention to write five short stories that could stand alone and also tie in together to form a complete full story. Together they'll be collected into a Keyport Cthulhu eBook and print version and run over 50,000 words, which I felt was more than enough to tell this story.

But then a strange thing happened… Keyport would not go away. Even after finishing the last line and sitting back from my desk I knew this was only the beginning to the real story… I already have an idea for another tale, this time most likely a novel length story I'll begin writing sometime in 2014… I hope you'll want to come back and read more about this quirky and dangerous little fishing village on the coast of New Jersey… but stay out of the cellars, please.

Author's Notes – Expanded Edition

Remember that 2014 novel idea I had? Still not working on it. Alas, other things come first like contracts and owning a podcast group (Project Entertainment Network… you should look it up. Some great podcasts on there).

Instead, I gave the original edition of this book an overhaul of sorts. Thanks to Chuck Buda and his passion for the short tales I wrote as well as the tie-in shorts (because I can never truly stop writing tales set in Keyport or of Cthulhu) we had a chat at a convention and the idea was born for him to write me a story.

Chuck wrote two, both of which are included in this expanded edition.

We also talked about someday doing a proper collaboration about a prequel to *Keyport Cthulhu*.

After all… there was a lot of story and history well before the events you just read…

I imagine if Chuck keeps the thought in my head long enough and he's as passionate about a prequel as he was about this re-release, you'll see it sooner than later…

Armand Rosamilia

March 2017

Armand Rosamilia is a New Jersey boy currently living in sunny Florida. He has a bunch of releases out and hopes to keep adding more until he stops. Simple as that. He loves meeting new people, so find him on Facebook or on Twitter (@ArmandAuthor) or his website, http://armandrosamilia.com

Katelynn Rosamilia Katelynn Rosamilia is a sixteen year old sophomore born in Red Bank, New Jersey and currently living in Florida. She has a passion for writing and has one novel published as well as a short story. She began writing at a young age and has loved it ever since.

Chuck Buda is a horror author from New Jersey. Growing up in Matawan, Chuck used to go to Keyport to eat fish and shop for Sunday school shoes. During his high school years, Chuck frequented some weird locations in Keyport.

Armand Rosamilia's *Keyport Cthulhu* became a sort of homecoming for Chuck. He quickly fell in love with Armand's mythos and setting. And getting the chance to be a part of this WORK OF ART is an honor, for which Chuck will forever be grateful.

You can find Chuck Buda anywhere throughout the state of New Jersey. Or you can follow him on Amazon: amazon.com/author/chuckbuda

The original *Keyport Cthulhu* cover, also by Jeffrey Kosh

Made in the USA
Monee, IL
02 July 2021